"You're torturing me..."

It was time to take control of the situation. But when Rick turned to face Jessie, he found her standing there unabashedly naked, her slim hands on those curvy hips, and his control slid through his veins in a snapping trail of sparks.

Double damn, she was the sexiest thing he'd ever seen. And with every moment of their last encounter replaying in his mind like a forbidden sex video, he doubted he would get through this night without sinking into her body one more time. Maybe three.

"You see, Sheriff, what you've been doing is torturing *me* with that sour mood all day. Now it seems as if I'm going to have to put up with it for another day or two."

Tossing condoms onto the bed like a little pile of promises, she casually crossed the room and flicked on the light.

"Personally," she went on, "the only time I happen to like you is when I've got my legs wrapped around your waist. So if I've got to deal with you all day, the least you can do is pleasure me at night...."

Dear Reader,

What is it about a wounded hero that makes us love him so much? Maybe it's the nurturer in us that makes us yearn to fix what's broken. Or maybe we simply love a challenge. Whatever the reason, there's something inherently intriguing about a man in need of emotional rescue and that one special woman who brings him hope.

When Rick Marshall sets his sights on Jessica Beane, he feels he's not capable of giving more than a one-night stand. But when circumstances push them together for an extended weekend, she manages to show him he's got plenty of living still to do.

I hope you have as much fun reading the story as I did writing it. Please drop me a note and tell me what you think of it. You can contact me through my Web site at www.LoriBorrill.com or mail me in care of Harlequin Books, 225 Duncan Mill Road, Don Mills, Ontario M3B 3K9, Canada.

Happy reading!

Lori Borrill

UNLEASHED
Lori Borrill

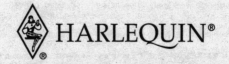

TORONTO • NEW YORK • LONDON
AMSTERDAM • PARIS • SYDNEY • HAMBURG
STOCKHOLM • ATHENS • TOKYO • MILAN • MADRID
PRAGUE • WARSAW • BUDAPEST • AUCKLAND

ISBN-13: 978-0-373-79434-8
ISBN-10:   0-373-79434-7

UNLEASHED

ABOUT THE AUTHOR

An Oregon native, Lori Borrill moved to the Bay Area just out of high school and has been a transplanted Californian ever since. Her weekdays are spent at the insurance company where's she's been employed for over twenty years, and she credits her writing career to the unending help and support she receives from her husband and real-life hero. When not sitting in front of a computer, she can usually be found at the Little League fields playing proud parent to their son. She'd love to hear from readers and can be reached through her Web site at www.LoriBorrill.com.

Books by Lori Borrill

HARLEQUIN BLAZE
308—PRIVATE CONFESSIONS
344—UNDERNEATH IT ALL
392—PUTTING IT TO THE TEST

1

"So, Sheriff, shall I spread 'em?"

Rick Marshall grasped the hips of the fiery redhead who had splayed her hands against the bedroom wall of his San Francisco flat.

"I'm thinking you should probably frisk me," she added, tossing a sinful wink over her shoulder and wiggling her bottom against his waist. "I could have something dangerous under my skirt."

He leaned in, pressing his lips close to the silky curls at her nape and whispered, "I'm counting on it."

She chuckled and he caught a whiff of something sweet. Peaches or strawberries. Or maybe it was the cherry she'd been sucking on back at the bar. The one she'd teased him with from across the room, trailing her tongue around the slick, red orb while sending him a look that said she'd prefer it if the cherry were his cock.

Rick normally wasn't such an easy mark, but between a crap day on the force and a couple condoms growing dust in his wallet, he decided not to play his usual game of not-interested. He'd found a spicy little Texan with her heart set on partying. Tonight was a night to do something he hadn't done in a long, long time.

Have some fun.

She brushed her ass against his crotch and his jeans strained against a cock that wanted to take this way too fast.

"Easy, Jess," he whispered into her ear. "This dick you're teasing hasn't seen much action lately." He slid his hands down her hips and held her steady. "I'd hate for this night to end before it gets started."

She spun around and pressed her back to the wall, the toying look in her eyes darkening to something serious while her hands went to work on his belt. "Right. I'm supposed to believe a tall, handsome man in uniform doesn't get any action?" She curved her mouth just short of a smile. "Don't let the drawl mistake me for stupid."

Oh, Jessica Beane most definitely wasn't stupid. He wouldn't have brought her home if she was. Despite the turned-up freckled nose and occasional girlish grin, the woman at work on his pants had eyes of experience, though what kind he wasn't sure. He only knew she wasn't naive or foolish, and for tonight, that's all he needed.

"Believe whatever turns you on," he said before covering her mouth with his.

Cupping her cheek with his hand, he dug in and feasted on the petite little beauty. She tasted like honey, felt like pure heaven and the surge to his pulse told him he needed this encounter more than he'd realized. Too much lately, he'd wrapped himself up in the job, every waking moment, every rampant thought devoted to getting creeps off the street. Since Nat's death, catching bad guys had gone from a job to an obsession he couldn't overcome, even though he knew that for every punk he brought in a dozen more were lined up after. It was a never-ending battle—he knew that—but it didn't stop the gnawing in his gut that kept him going. Working homicide, he'd seen too many of those blank stares, the eyes of the dead, silently begging him to catch one more.

And you caught them all too late, didn't you, pal?

He sucked in a heavy breath, inhaling the spicy fragrance of Jessie's hair, breathing deeply to extinguish the haunting voice. Sliding his hands toward her breasts, he needed to touch and absorb something living, something soft, vital and whole. He needed this escape, this heated rush of blood through his veins to remind himself that he was still among the living, that there was still pleasure to be found in this sometimes dark world. And before this night was over, he intended to find lots of it. He hadn't walked into Scotty's looking for sex, but he'd found it in this red-hot cowgirl. And as she won the battle with his belt and went to work on his fly, he thanked Jessica Beane and her sinful cherries. A one-night stand was exactly what the doctor ordered.

With increased fury, she unfastened the buttons on his 501's while their mouths licked and sucked.

Wondering why the rush, he came up for breath. "You in a hurry to get somewhere?"

"Yeah. In your pants."

He kissed a path to her ear. "I mean after that." Grasping her left hand, he jiggled her ring finger. "You don't need to get home to someone, do you?"

He could sense the roll of her eyes in her voice. "No ring. No husband." Then she huffed and added, "No boyfriend, no partner, no significant other. Not even a crush on a movie star."

"Good," he said. "Because I'd like to keep you for a while." Tasting the base of her neck, he slipped a hand up under her black, sleeveless T-shirt and grabbed hold of a breast covered in something silky. A hard nipple topped the mound, and when he brushed his thumb over the smooth nub, her soft moan vibrated against his lips.

"This is nice," he said, sliding his spare hand up her shirt to toy with the other mound. He circled his palms over her nipples where they tickled his skin and sent sparks through his veins.

Her hands tugged at his jeans, the brush of her fingers against his length hardening an already threatening erection. He'd gone too long without the taste of a woman, erroneously thinking that a quick jerk-off in the shower could replace this feeling of flesh against flesh. Her mere touch was enough to send him careening toward the edge. So when she released his goods and took his hard, naked shaft in her hand, he quickly grabbed her forearms and pulled away.

"Babe, I wasn't joking. You're playing with a man overdue." Guiding her hands around his waist instead, he trailed his tongue against her earlobe. "I'd like this evening to last a while."

She responded by sliding to her knees. "Then we should take the edge off."

Every nerve in his body went on alert when those soft, wet lips touched his cock and cloaked him in slick warmth. The blood in his brain rushed south, stiffening his shaft until it throbbed.

"Babe, don't," he attempted, trying to pull from her mouth, when she relented, grabbing his ass and running her smooth tongue all the way from tip to base.

"Relax and go with it," she urged, but the anxious beauty didn't know what she was dealing with. She probably thought she'd come home with a regular guy. Someone who had real, live sex on a regular basis and who could shoot his wad and bounce back sometime before dawn for a few more rounds.

And on another day he would have been that man.

But he'd had too many sleepless nights, and the sensations boiling through him had been too long coming. He was overheating, the climax threatening to hit with such force he'd be spent for sure.

He may have lost most everything in his life, but he still had his pride.

She grabbed his balls and licked, and now he really did try to pull away. Until she opened wide and took him in fully.

Weeks of stress and tension slipped from his neck and shoulders, spilling down his back and sliding over his legs until his knees went weak and he had to brace himself against the wall. He cursed. Her wicked, hardheaded intent that had intrigued him in the bar was about to do him in right here. And as she clasped his hips and began motioning him to thrust his cock inside her, he lost the will to fight.

For the moment he simply obeyed, her moans of pleasure filling his ears and draining his mind of everything but the slick, tight feel of her tongue caressing his shaft. And as he let his body take over, pumping in and out while her fingers toyed with his ass, her groans played like music in the quiet of his room.

Electricity rushed through him, curling his fingers against the smooth, plastered wall, sounding a hum in his chest that erupted in one last warning.

"Jessica, I mean it. This is—" But a sharp stab of sensation sped up from his cock, trapping the words in his throat.

"Oh, yeah," she murmured before taking him in deep, apparently recognizing the signals that he was about to burst.

The waves kept sweeping through him, each one heavier than the last, and quickly his consciousness drained of everything but the feel of that mouth sucking hard on his flesh. His body lurched, his sight fading to black, his ears numbing to silence as the swirling cyclone of sensation began at the base of his spine and moved slowly toward the apex.

He leaned closer, his elbows scraping against the wall as he widened his stance in an attempt to brace himself for the crash, but before he could get a grip, she pressed a finger to the sensitive spot behind his balls and everything in him exploded.

"Oh, sh—" he cried out, bucking and jerking against her. His cock began to slip from her lips and she latched on, holding him in, dragging that tongue across his length and spreading white heat through every cell in his body.

He came hard, then came again, the waves ripping through him in a constant barrage of swell and release. For what seemed like an eternity he simply gave in to the motion, his flesh and her will taking over, holding him captive and sending him to places unknown. He didn't know how long it went on before the light slowly returned and her sweet sound of satisfaction filled his ears.

She was still on her knees, her tongue still caressing his shaft when he'd finally regained the motor skills to push from the wall and stand erect.

And then mortification swept through him. He hadn't had the woman in his bedroom for more than ten minutes before he'd humped her like a dog in heat and came in her mouth. What the hell was wrong with him?

Taking quick hold of her arms, he helped her to her feet, those sexy brown eyes expressing nothing but hot, ripe desire. Still, he opened his mouth to utter a lame apology, not knowing what to say or where to start. But before he could try, she whipped her black T-shirt over her head exposing two beautiful, round breasts covered in green silk and lace.

He stood dumbfounded as she wiggled out of her skirt, leaving her clad only in a matching thong and two sharp black stilettos.

A circle of moisture darkened the spot between her legs, underscoring her remark, "That was ridiculously hot."

It was an understatement.

She stepped from the pooled skirt at her feet and moved toward him, slow and deliberate, stopping for a moment to slide a finger between her legs then touch it to her lips. "Yes," she said. "That definitely got me going."

He swallowed.

When she reached him, she trailed the wet finger over his mouth as she stood close and eyed his lips intently. "Want a taste?"

Now her sweet honey scent was laced with sweat and sex, and as she rubbed her body against his, all the spots he'd feared might sleep for the night woke up for another round.

"Unbelievable," he muttered, sucking the slick tip of her finger into his mouth. Though she was a virtual stranger, she managed to know his body better than he knew it himself.

Or did she simply know her own capabilities?

Either way, she'd read him perfectly. He had needed to take the edge off, because now his pulse strummed with a tempered warmth that allowed him to relax and enjoy the seduction.

Straddling one leg, she pressed her sex to his thigh and began rocking against him, moving her hips in a dance, a slick spot growing where her clit met the fabric of his jeans. She moistened her lips and watched as he flicked his tongue against her finger, gliding it back and forth over the tip, demonstrating exactly what he planned to do to more sensitive spots on her body.

"That's it," she said. "That's exactly how I want it."

And the cock he'd thought was spent hardened as if they'd just gotten started.

He whipped her into his arms and tossed her on the bed, still awash in wonder over how this woman managed to tip him so far so quickly. Before tonight, he'd feared himself too old, tired and ruined for sex like this. But as he pulled the thong down her waist and began feasting, the years and sleepless nights slipped away, leaving him as pumped and virile as he'd been back before his life had fallen apart.

She crooked the heel of her shoe against one shoulder then did the same with the other, leaving her wide and exposed to receive all the gracious pleasure she'd given moments ago. And as he dove in, he thanked Fate for bringing him this momentary respite.

Not a drinker, he rarely went into the bars, much less picked up a playmate for the evening. They were usually more trouble than they were worth, expecting more than he could give.

Which was pretty much nothing.

But something seemed to be propelling him tonight. Like the tide carries a bottle from one shore to another, ever since he left the station he seemed to be succumbing to a force stronger than his will. And as he began the slow climb toward another searing climax, he opted to go with it rather than question it, for once relishing this life that had somehow gone out of his control.

"SO WHAT WAS IT you were celebrating again?" Rick asked under the soft glow of the lone lamp that rested on his bedside table. Jessie had snuggled against him, her dimpled chin digging into his chest, sheets draped haphazardly around her waist while she trailed a finger over his abs.

Her eyes lit with a smile and she bolted from the bed. Excitement bounced in her steps as she shot out a quick, "I'll show you," before disappearing into the front room.

Where she got the energy, he'd never know. Though he'd discovered far more stamina than he believed he had, three hours of sex had officially drained every muscle in his body. The way he felt right now, brushing lint from his arm would be a stretch. Yet there was Jessica Beane, her perpetual beat leaving him wondering if she had a point of exhaustion.

Settling back next to him, she propped against a pillow and held up a worn and wrinkled copy of *People* magazine. Pointing to a celebrity photograph, she proudly exclaimed, "That."

He squinted to find the significance under the dim light.

"Jewel Murray?" he asked, vaguely remembering the name of the blond starlet pictured strolling across a street.

"No, that," Jessie replied, moving her slim finger to the handbag the actress was carrying. It was bright pink, adorned with shiny black sequins and—*were those green feathers?*

Jessie beamed, "It's a Beane Bag. This photo just made me famous."

A sliver of their bar conversation came back to him, something about the fact that she made designer handbags for a living—or was trying to. She was part of a co-op of struggling artists who owned a boutique on the edge of Union Square.

"Would you believe I was down to my last three hundred

dollars when this photo appeared in *People?*" she went on. "I was actually canvassing the neighborhood looking for another job. That's how I found Scotty's. They'd posted an ad for a waitress and I liked the fact that it's a hangout for cops." She eyed him with all innocence. "Safer, you know?"

He nearly laughed out loud. Sure, cops typically upheld the law, but put a few together with a couple of cocktails after an especially tough day and any woman intent on keeping her pants on could hardly consider herself safe.

He decided not to burst her bubble.

"I'd just accepted a part-time shift at IHOP when this photo hit the stands," she said. "It took twenty-four hours before stores all over the country were calling me for inventory. I even got a call from Paris. *Paris,* can you believe it?"

No, but her excitement was contagious. Those caramel eyes had a way of sucking him in, beaming so brightly with delight he couldn't help but feel a little thrill for her.

She hopped up to her knees and clutched the magazine to her chest like it was her most prized possession. "I was able to get a loan from the bank. Just enough to cover supplies on order and hire myself an assistant." Her grin widened. "I'm still in a daze. One minute, I'm going to be a waitress at IHOP and the next I'm hiring assistants to help me make purses I'll be shipping to Paris."

With a bounce to every move, she tucked the magazine into her purse and slid back into bed. "So, yeah, I'm celebrating." She swung a leg over his waist and straddled his lap. Her girlish innocence darkened to pure woman as she traced a finger over his lips, eyeing them as if she were imagining what he might do with them. "And you're the lucky guy who gets to celebrate with me."

Unbelievably a wave of heat hardened his cock.

Moments ago, with her curled up beside him and every part of his body tucked in for the night, he'd doubted a typhoon could have gotten him to stir. Yet all it had taken was a wiggle of Jessie's round, little bottom, the crush of her breasts against his chest and that sneaky look of sex in her copper-kettle eyes to get his body buzzing all over again.

Just when he thought he'd broken the record on marathon sex, he found the will to sink into her one more time, to drive his tired, sated body to one last brink and beyond.

And that's exactly what he did. One more taste of that sweet, supple body. One more sweep of life through his veins. One more climb to the tip of ecstasy and one last crash into the abyss.

And when they were done, he slipped into the longest, deepest sleep he'd enjoyed in as many years as he could remember.

2

THE RING of her phone stirred Jessie from what had been a light and restless sleep. Not that she was troubled. On the contrary, she felt like a kid on Christmas Eve, excitement and anticipation keeping her too pumped up for anything more than a turbulent doze.

Granna Hawley had been right. Get out of Texas and all the bad luck that had plagued her life would come to an end. And if Jessie had doubted her paternal grandmother before, these last few days proved the woman had been right. Life had definitely been on the upswing since she'd stepped off the plane in San Francisco, the latest in her run of good fortune being an incredible night of sex with the gorgeous cop beside her.

Rolling off the bed, she grabbed her purse and his charcoal-gray T-shirt and headed for the front room, wanting to close the door behind her before the phone woke him. Although, looking over the broad mound, she doubted a hurricane would pull the man from sleep. Every inch of him was crushed against the big bed, those sharp, chiseled features sunk so deeply into his pillow she had to do a double take to see if he was actually breathing. Only when her phone sounded again, prompting the slight twitch of his right index finger, did she turn and step out of the room, satisfied her handsome lover hadn't slipped into a sex-induced coma.

The thought made her smile, and as she flipped open the phone, the memory of the last few hours brought a layer of steam to her voice.

"Hello?"

"So you *are* alive."

It was her friend and roommate, Georgia. "Of course, I'm alive, though when my strong and studly sheriff wakes up from his nap, I might be indisposed."

Georgia didn't sound impressed. "You forgot the rule."

"What rule?"

"I'm serious, Jessie, if you can't remember the rules, I'm not letting you go home with strangers."

The giddy smile wilted from Jessie's face as she recalled the drilling she'd received from Georgia earlier that evening, before the two women stepped out for the bars. "I was supposed to call."

"Ding-ding-ding-ding! We have a winner."

Still clutching Rick's T-shirt in her hand, she pressed it to her forehead and lowered to his couch. "I'm sorry," she replied, her voice muffled through fabric that smelled deliciously like musk and man.

"I'll give you a break this time because it's your first pickup date, but I'm serious. If you want to play the cosmopolitan woman, you've got to think like one, and that includes remembering that you're not in Tulouse, Texas, anymore."

And wasn't Jessie thankful for that? Not that she had a problem with cowboys. She'd heard plenty of favorable stories about the rugged men on the range. It was just that the men in Tulouse were more *boy* than cowboy, and especially after this evening, she'd take the dangers of the big city over what she'd found back home.

"Tell me where you are so I can forget my miserable evening and go to bed."

"What happened to the blond, beautiful beat cop you were hanging on to when Rick and I left?"

"Beat cop was right. He *beat* me to the orgasm then took off before I could even work up a decent flush." Jessie heard the crunch of a taco chip through the phone—a sure sign Georgia wasn't exaggerating about her miserable evening. She always drowned a bad day in a bag of Doritos. "Tell me your night went better than mine."

Jessie smiled as she recalled the events of the evening, starting with the stormy look of intent in Rick's sizzling blue eyes and ending with her desperate cries of release as she'd dug her fingers through his thick, dark hair and climaxed one last time. Still she tempered her excitement for the sake of her friend. "Marathon Man," she said. "If I wasn't so excited about my meetings tomorrow, I'd be dead to the world like he is."

"Beginner's luck," Georgia droned.

Could be, but Jessie knew it was more than that. It was Georgia who had convinced her to take Granna Hawley's advice—and inheritance—and come out to San Francisco. And once she got here, it was Georgia who taught her how to put herself ahead of everyone else. Lesson one being to stop looking at men as potential husbands and start using them for what they're good for: sex and vehicle maintenance.

Okay, so maybe Georgia's ideals were soured by one too many jerks, but Jessie had to admit a certain liberation in having sex with a man she had no intention of getting serious with. For the first time ever, she abandoned concern over making a good impression and decided to go for broke.

And in the process left her dark and sexy companion completely and utterly spent.

Perhaps it was beginner's luck that she'd found a man who could keep up with her. Or perhaps it was that, away from her hometown roots, she'd had the nerve to step into the driver's seat and have the kind of sex she'd always wanted. Either way, this newfound freedom was working, giving Jessica Beane yet another reason to be thrilled with the new life she'd been given.

"I'll take luck however it comes," she said, prompting Georgia to finally laugh.

"Hon, you deserve a good time after everything you've been through." Another crunch and Georgia added, "Now tell me where you are so I can send you back to Marathon Man and put an end to my own disastrous evening."

"Hold on a sec," Jessie said, trying to remember where exactly Rick's two-story flat was. She recalled turning off Nineteenth Avenue, but that was about it. There'd been an Asian market down the block, but she'd forgotten the name, and with an Asian market on every street in San Francisco, that wouldn't help her.

Her sexy sheriff had driven all the way from Scotty's with one hand up her skirt, and by the time they'd turned down his street all she could think about was how many steps to the bedroom door. Street names and house numbers were just a lusty blur. Still, she and Georgia had a pact. If they went home with a new beau, they were to call each other with addresses just to be safe.

Something Jessie had completely forgotten about while she and Rick were testing the limits of sexual acrobatics.

Pulling his shirt over her head, she was pleased to see the hem nearly reach her knees. No surprise since the man had more than a foot on her five-foot-two frame. But it helped that she wouldn't have to go back to the bedroom in search of her underwear, and after picking up the phone from the couch, she crossed the front room and opened the drapes of the large window that faced the street.

A wall of two-story row houses lined the opposite side of the street, each one painted a bright pastel, some topped with clay tile roofs, others adorned with iron balconies. All had single-car garages on the ground floor next to wide stucco stairways leading to the top-floor entry. Ornate iron gates guarded each doorway, and grand bay windows hung like turrets over the garages, providing an unobstructed view of the public sidewalk below.

It was the picture of just about every street in San Francisco.

She looked one way, then the other. "I can't see the street name from here. I think I'm in the middle of a block."

"Missing Persons will probably want more information than that."

Jessie scowled but relented. She'd gone home with a cop for heaven's sake, but Georgia had always told her to stay aware of her surroundings and never trust a soul.

Advice she could have used long before she moved to San Francisco.

Making her way to the front door, she unlocked the dead bolt and the latch on the painted white gate and stepped outside, finally locating both the street name and house numbers and relaying them to her friend.

"See how easy that was?" Georgia asked. "Now, if you show up missing, someone knows where you went. Congratulations, you've just passed your first course in Casual Sexual Encounters, albeit you've barely squeaked by with a C minus."

Jessie laughed. "I'll be home earlier than later. Remember, I've got interviews with assistants in the morning."

Just saying the words sent a shiver up her spine. Her Assistants. *Her assistants.* She was actually going to own a business…with employees.

"Swan will be opening the shop. If one of your candidates gets there before you, I'm sure she'll keep the girl rapt by showing off her latest in Native American jewelry."

Chuckling, Jessie said goodbye and tossed the phone in her purse, the conversation a reminder that she really should still try to get some sleep. She'd never interviewed anyone for a job before, and she wanted to be clearheaded enough to make the right choice. So after making a quick stop in the bathroom, she headed back to the bedroom to do that when her phone rang again.

She picked it up and huffed. "Yes, dear?"

"Was he good?"

The low, familiar voice slithered through her veins like ice, trapping the air in her lungs and freezing her feet to the cold wood floor.

She opened her mouth and tried to speak, but the only thing that came out was a low gurgle.

"Aw, c'mon, Sugar. When a woman cheats on her husband, the least she can do is share the gory details." She heard the draw of a cigarette before she added, through an exhale, "Is pretty cop-boy good in bed?"

Her heart thumped and her knees buckled causing her

to brace a hand to the back of the couch. A hundred questions spun in a flurry of disbelief, blurring her thoughts and reducing her words to a stutter.

Rounding the couch, she slowly lowered to one arm. "Wa-Wade?"

"Well, since you forgot that I'm your husband, I'm glad you at least remembered my name."

She blinked and sputtered then finally managed to hiss, "You're not my husband." Not that that was the primary thought going through her head right now. She just wanted him to stop saying it.

More importantly, she wondered how he got her cell phone number, why he was calling her and *how did he know where she was?*

The thought put her feet in motion and she scampered to the front window, peering down to the street below. There were cars parallel parked up and down the quiet avenue, but other than that, it looked deserted in the wee hour of the night.

She heard him blow out another puff of smoke and she darted her eyes back and forth before seeing an old battered pickup parked two doors down in front of a pale yellow stucco. The windows on the truck were fogged and she caught a faint puff of smoke escape from the driver's side.

"Yeah, well, that's where you're wrong, Sugar. You and I are still entirely conjugated."

"You're in jail," she whispered, hoping that saying the words out loud would make it true.

"Not anymore, Sugar Beane. And I've come all the way to California to reunite with my loving bride."

"Stop calling me that! I'm not your wife. You signed the divorce papers in jail."

"You know, I should be angry," he said through another drag of his cigarette. "Coming all this way only to find my woman leaving a bar with another man. You're lucky I'm not the jealous type."

Coward was more like it, but she shook the remark from her thoughts. She needed to stay focused.

"Most men would be barging up there with a shotgun."

She snapped her eyes to the truck. "You—" was all she could utter.

Had Wade ever handled a gun? She didn't think so, but then again, there'd been a lot of things she hadn't known about Wade Griggs up until a year ago.

His laugh was raspy and cold. "I'll forgive you as long as you give me the same favors you gave Officer Hard-On there." Another suck off his butt and he added, "You always were the best at giving head."

A wave of nausea stumbled her back a step. The image of her and Wade—

She cupped a hand over her mouth and tried to block it from her thoughts. No way would she let that animal turn something beautiful she'd shared with a deserving man into the dirt and grime he crawled from.

"My cock's getting hard just thinking about—"

She snapped the phone shut and tossed it on the couch as though it were a grenade about to explode. Her desire to run from it underscored the feeling. Her heart raced, her hands went clammy, and as she glanced over the dark shadows of the room, she went dizzy with disgust and confusion.

What was Wade Griggs doing here? Why wasn't he in jail? And if he was released, why hadn't anyone called to tell her?

And then the big question: What did he want from her?

She and Wade were through. They were through the

moment the cops had shown up at her house and informed her that the body shop she and her husband owned was a front for a car theft ring. That her husband was being indicted for grand theft auto. That she was considered an accessory until proven innocent. And that everything they owned was being seized by the county, the state and the Internal Revenue Service.

He'd lied to her from the start, her trust in him landing her in a pile of trouble so deep it took every last cent she had to get out of it. As such, she was left with nothing more than a quick divorce and a bad credit rating.

He'd drained her of everything, and less than twelve months later he was back—wanting what?

The phone rang again, and she reluctantly picked it up, her fingers trembling and tears threatening at the backs of her eyes.

This can't be happening. *Not now.*

She pressed the phone to her ear in time to hear the end of "…used to love it when I talked dirty—"

"What do you *want?*" she snarled.

"I told you, Sugar Beane. I came to find my wife."

"I'm not your wife." How many times did she have to repeat it?

"Now, that's where you're mistaken, honey cakes. You see, that divorce you set up never got finished."

She blinked, her nausea easing into simple confusion.

"What are you talking about?"

"You and I are still blissfully wed, Sugar Beane. And that means everything that's yours is mine."

She stood up and stepped back to the window, this time to find Wade standing casually at the rear bumper of a red Honda Accord parked directly across the street.

"You're wrong."

Though he was one story down and across the wide street, she could see the rough-edged smile on his long, narrow face. He was tall and more bulky than she'd remembered. His jeans bagged around his boots and the button-down shirt made him appear more kept than usual, even though his right shirttail hung over his leather belt.

He'd apparently dressed himself up for the reunion.

"Check your papers, darlin'. You don't have anything signed by me."

Of course, she did. Though not recalling offhand exactly where the papers were allowed an inkling of panic to creep in.

She remembered specifically having them drawn up, signing them in her lawyer's office and having them couriered to the county jail. She remembered that day as if it was yesterday. She'd signed them. They'd been notarized. Wade had signed them, too.

Hadn't he?

"Things got a little hectic back then, what with Old Lady Hawley up and dying like that," he drawled.

She squeezed her eyes shut. No, no, no. This was Wade playing games with her. He signed those papers. She knew it as well as she knew her own name. "The lawyer called and said you'd signed," she contended, though a tremble in her voice watered down the affirmation.

"You sure about that? Are you sure you aren't thinking about the call you got from that lawyer telling you old Granna Hawley left you all her money?"

Her eyes shot open and she glared at him through the window.

"Half of which is mine, you realize."

Shaking her head, Jessie thought about the time, through a fever of distress and ire. The lawyer *did* call. She'd gotten the package in the mail. She was sure of it.

Wasn't she?

A slow swell of bile rose up her throat. She'd signed those papers the day before Granna Hawley died. Sure, she'd been devastated by the loss. Gran was the only person Jessie could ever count on. And then there'd been the funeral arrangements and the impending feud between her father's side of the family and her mother's—the former insisting the latter had no business anywhere near the cemetery. It had been a mess, with Jessica slammed right in the center.

But in the middle of it, she knew Wade had signed those divorce papers. The lawyers told her so. The package came in the mail.

She was sure that it had….

The bile hit the back of her mouth and she nearly choked. All these doubts, this was Wade and his games. He'd gotten out of jail and come here just to screw with her. He was only feeding his own sick sense of humor, hoping to get her back for dumping him the moment she'd learned the truth about him.

"We're divorced," she said again, this time with more velocity than the last.

"My lawyer says you got almost a hundred thousand dollars from the old woman after taxes. Plus half of that ten thousand you just borrowed."

Her mouth fell open.

"Yeah, as your husband I know all about your finances."

"Then you know I don't have any of that money anymore."

"No. And you don't have the five hundred dollars you'd

stashed in that black velvet box, either." He patted his back pocket. "Consider it your first installment."

He'd been in her apartment?

And if he'd rummaged through the place, how much had he found? She had Granna's jewelry and Grandpa Hawley's watch.

Georgia had a diamond ring that belonged to her mother. She cherished that thing. Had Wade found that, too?

She nearly doubled over. If her friend lost anything thanks to that snake, she'd never forgive herself.

"I'm disappointed, Sugar Beane. I came all this way looking for my wife and my money only to find you broke and in bed with another man. Now, what do you think a husband should do about that?"

Clutching the phone so hard she thought it might snap, she repeated through clenched teeth. "You're not my husband."

"Oh, yes, I am. And as your husband, you owe me somewheres in the neighborhood of fifty thousand dollars." He pushed off the fender of the Honda and stood straight, the smile drained from his face and his eyes black as sin. "Get me the money, Sugar Beane, and you can have your divorce."

"I already have my divorce, and even if I don't, I don't have that kind of money. It's gone. Sunk into my business."

"Yeah, your momma told me all about that movie star who's gonna make you famous. I'm looking forward to sharing half your wealth." Then flashing a grin she could see all the way from the street, he added, "Now, why don't you come down and share a little of that sweet ass, too? Or am I not as worthy as your fuck buddy?"

She snapped the phone shut then turned it off, not willing to hear anymore.

Wade was wrong. They were divorced. And the moment

she got home, she'd find those papers and prove that she had nothing to worry about.

Scattering about the dark space, she went in search of her things. Rick was still sprawled like a stone tablet across his bed, the slow rise of his back the only indication he was still breathing.

Moments ago, she'd been on top of the world, this sexy, chiseled cop sending her to all kinds of heavenly places and leaving her feeling like a queen. And with one phone call, her past had come crashing back, storming through the gates of her new life like an angry mob intent on raping and pillaging everything she'd created.

Clenched fists at her sides, she vowed not to let it happen. She wasn't sweet, little Sugar Beane anymore, dumb and ignorant and ready to roll over for every con artist who crossed her path. Her tryst with Rick underscored that. Here in California she was an independent, grown woman capable of taking on the world, and no car-stealing felon of an ex-husband was going to topple her now.

For a second, she considered waking up Rick and sending him downstairs to throw Wade back behind bars where he belonged, but she quickly extinguished the thought. It was time she stopped believing anyone would come to her rescue. In her twenty-seven years, Granna Hawley was the only person she'd ever been able to lean on, who'd stood up for her and defended her when she needed someone in her corner. That made one person among a half-dozen family members who should have helped but only disappointed—Wade Griggs being the last in a long line of them.

How she could think a practical stranger would come to her aid only proved she hadn't yet wised up, so instead of waking him, she quickly threw on her clothes, grabbed her purse and took off out the back alley. She ran up the street, only stopping to call a cab after she was blocks away from Wade and his threats.

She needed to take care of this herself. And as soon as she got home and found the papers she knew were there, she'd succeed in sending Wade Griggs right back to the swill he came from. Doing so would be a message to everyone that Jessica Beane couldn't be screwed with ever again.

3

A SHARP BLADE of sunlight slipped between the drapes in Rick's bedroom and stretched across his face, drawing him from deep sleep into a groggy morning haze.

He blinked his eyes open and winced. He wasn't accustomed to being woken by sunlight, his unsteady dreams usually pulling him from bed long before dawn. But last night there were no dreams, just an intoxicating blend of soft woman and hard sleep.

Angling his head away from the deadly light ray, he tried opening his eyes again, curious to know exactly how late he'd slept. The red digital numbers on his clock said seven forty-five. A record. At least, one he hadn't broken in…he tried to recall…

Exactly two years, eight months and two weeks, give or take a couple days.

He clamped his eyes shut, not interested in letting his thoughts take over and ruin the restful climax to one hell of an evening. Especially when there were better ways to start the day.

Rolling over, he reached for the sexy cowgirl responsible for his divine night of slumber, trying to decide which parting gift he'd like to leave her with. Several came to mind. All of them involving her legs around his neck. But when he slid a hand over the mattress, he came up with nothing but sheet. He felt the pillows, flat and cold, before opening his eyes and propping up on an elbow. The bed was definitely empty, and glancing around the dim room, he noted the rest of the master suite was empty, too.

Was she down the hall making coffee? That would be too blissful to imagine. A smile quirked his mouth as he envisioned the petite, sexy redhead slipping back into bed with two mugs of black coffee and steam in her eyes. But when he rolled on his back and allowed his mind and body to slowly wake, the house felt awfully quiet.

Frowning, he tossed his legs over the side of the bed and scratched his chest, still trying to capture his bearings. His clothes were scattered across the tan carpet, as were a number of foil condom wrappers—little remnants of a night well spent. A pillow had found its way to the foot of his stuffy sofa chair, and he wondered how it got there until the memory made him smile.

Oh, Ms. Beane, you know how to have a good time.

He shoved off the bed and began collecting the wrappers, counting them as he went until it occurred to him everything that belonged to Jessie was gone. The denim skirt she'd wiggled out of as he was still recovering from the first orgasm, the black strappy high heels she'd kicked off with her toes, the lacy green bra, the tight black T-shirt, the funky orange "Beane Bag," all stripped from the room as if last night had been nothing more than a dream.

He grabbed his pants and pulled them on, then crossed the room and opened the door. Stepping through his front room, down the hall to the kitchen past the bathroom and back, he came to terms with the fact that his spicy Texas lover was gone.

And for a long moment, he stood, trying to understand why that irked him.

Last night she'd been the answer to everything he'd needed just then, a lover that rivaled his every fantasy, fulfilling every horny desire and tossing out two or three more for good measure. Now this morning she'd gone the extra mile by adding one more favor. She'd taken off. No awkward goodbyes, no empty promises to call. She'd simply grabbed her things and left. And for a man already complicated by a hard past and a harder present, it was the sweetest move she could have made.

So why was he so pissed?

Padding back to the kitchen, he lifted the carafe of day-old coffee from the machine. He sniffed the contents and grimaced, but still opted to nuke a cup rather than brew a fresh pot. He was too disturbed by his own annoyance to fret over the quality of his morning's caffeine, and as he choked down the first bitter sip, he leaned against the counter and tried to talk some sense into himself.

What had he planned to do, ask for her number? Send her flowers and start taking her out for regular Friday-night dates? He'd made it clear before they'd left the bar that if she was looking for more than one fun evening, she'd need to keep trolling. She hadn't balked, and this morning, she'd proven that her indifference hadn't been an act. She'd truly meant what she'd said about wanting to keep things casual. There'd been no day-after confessions leading to guilty apologies and the ever-awkward, "Gee, I thought you'd understood…"

She'd wanted exactly what he'd wanted. They'd been a goddamn one-night match made in heaven. So standing here burned, since she'd one-upped him on her race for the door, seemed immature at best.

The rational thought helped only slightly. However, instead of spending the morning in his kitchen trying to analyze his feelings, he decided it was time to forget about it and head for the station.

Until a sharp knock at the entry had him thinking again. Stepping down the hall, he grabbed the knob and whipped open the door, but rather than finding his wily sex-starved bedmate, he found a short Chinese man with a bad haircut and a frown on his face.

"You forget you had a job?" his partner, Kevin Fong, grumbled as he pushed through the door and entered the flat, a cup of Starbucks in one hand. Kevin's angry look had Rick guessing he hadn't brought an extra cup for him.

Rick closed the door behind them. "It's barely eight."

"And when was the last time you showed up for work later than seven?" It hadn't been in the year and a half he and Kevin had been partners. "And when did you stop answering your cell phone?" Kevin added.

Rick glanced down at the mahogany side table where he could have sworn he'd tossed his car keys and cell phone the night before. "My phone?" he said absently, patting the pockets of his jeans then moving into the bedroom to look around.

Kevin followed, eyeing him suspiciously as he leaned in the doorway and took in the surroundings. "Captain's been trying to get hold of you all morning."

Rick stopped rummaging through the room and glanced at the clock. "It's seven fifty-five!"

"He's apparently a vampire like you." Kevin yawned. "Woke me up at an ungodly hour because he couldn't reach you. You've been my mission for the last hour."

Rick seriously needed a lesson in expectation management. Barely having a life was one thing. Having his boss call out the posse because he hadn't shown up for work *early* brushed the edge of illegal. "What's the captain doing working on a Saturday anyway?" he grumbled.

"Creed Thornton managed to get his property released from evidence," Kevin explained. "They're coming first thing this morning to pick up everything we seized from his condo."

"That's why I got to it yesterday." Rick went back to looking for his cell phone.

"Captain wants to know why you checked out his laptop." Then with an added layer of annoyance, Kevin added, "And since we're supposed to be working this case together, it might be nice if you told me, too."

"If you'd met me at Scotty's last night like you should have, you'd already know."

Kevin pulled a pen from his coat jacket, bent over and used it to lift Jessie's emerald-green thong out from behind his TV stand. "Looks like you ended up better off without me," he said, holding it up as if it were crime scene evidence.

Rick stepped over and yanked the panties away from his partner. He preferred his personal life stay personal, having had enough of it all over the news when his wife was killed. And the look he flashed Kevin said the man wasn't going to get the gory details he was looking for.

"Message delivered. Why don't you let me shower and get dressed and I'll meet you down at the station?"

"You forgot the part about filling me in on what you're doing with our murder investigation." Kevin moved in, kicked away the pillow from Rick's side chair and took a seat. "Why did you check out the laptop last night? The crime lab said it was clean."

"I want a second opinion."

Kevin laughed. "Not that smarmy hacker friend of yours from the Haight."

"He's not a friend."

"You aren't denying the smarmy part."

"He's better than the geek squad downtown."

Kevin conceded, knowing Rick was right. The crime lab was good at sniffing deleted files out of PCs and laptops. And on occasion they'd worked wonders tracing lines through the Internet and drumming up long-lost e-mails. But they weren't the be all and end all in computer hacking, and his "smarmy friend" in the Haight was.

"You realize nothing this guy finds will stand up in court. Any lead you get from it will get tossed out the minute a sharp lawyer discovers how you got it."

"Thank you for the lesson in criminal justice."

"I'm just sayin'…" He shrugged before taking a sip of his coffee.

"Yeah, and like you said, they're coming to pick up his evidence this morning. I've got a better chance with it in the hands of my hacker than back with a murderer." He stared hard at his partner before adding, "That laptop's the only chance we've got. This case is going cold, about to turn Arctic the minute Thornton's lawyers collect that computer this morning." He turned back to the bathroom and tossed over his shoulder, "Besides, you know as well as I do we can get around explaining how we come up with tips. We need to look again at what's on there, then worry about what to do with it."

"They're gonna be pissed when the laptop's not there. I get the feeling the captain's willing to cover your ass, but he needs an explanation before they show up looking for it."

That was the easy part. The laptop was their first break in nailing Creed Thornton for the murder of Anna Mendoza. And Rick had no doubt the man was responsible.

A hotshot software developer with rich parents and even richer in-laws, Creed's pampered life hit a snag when his maid turned up dead and pregnant with his child. Their explanation had been suicide, the poor girl so distraught that he refused to divorce his wife, she'd hanged herself in her own bathroom. But too many sides to that scenario weren't sitting well, most notably the smug composure of a man certain he was about to get away with murder.

Rick and Kevin had been chasing dead ends for months, every lead extinguished, every road ending up nowhere. In recent weeks, even Rick had come close to admitting that Paolo and Lucy Mendoza might never get justice for their daughter.

However, Creed had made the one mistake that could cost him his freedom. He wanted his evidence back. And he wanted it so badly that he'd sent his team of lawyers on an expensive and politically charged rampage to get every item they'd seized from his condo before week's end.

On news of that, Rick had taken inventory and come up with the item that seemed to be garnering too much attention—Creed's laptop. The urgency didn't make sense. The man was a software engineer with a dozen computers at his disposal. So why the sudden need to have this one—and fast? The crime lab found it clean, but Creed's company specialized in security encryption. He would be just cocky enough to test his programs in the most ultimate way—with his life.

And now, suddenly it was critical he get his hands back on the computer. Could it be second thoughts? Did he have newfound reservations that with an expert, his secrets might not be as safe as he'd presumed?

Rick wasn't sure, but he intended to find out.

"We'd all like to know what you're up to," Kevin said.

"Easy. Creed wants his laptop back and I want to know why the sudden interest."

Kevin rubbed his chin like he always did when he was thinking, taking the look in Rick's eyes and coming up with the same conclusion. It was one reason Rick appreciated Kevin more than he had any other partner during his fifteen years on the force.

Though only two years in homicide and still learning the ropes, Kevin caught on fast. He was sharp and meticulous, sniffing out facts while Rick shot from the cuff and followed hunches. Their opposing styles seemed to strike a balance that worked well for both Rick and the force. Now they just needed it to work well for this murder case, too.

"Has Smarmy Friend found anything yet?" Kevin asked.

"He doesn't have the laptop yet. I'm meeting him this morning at ten to drop it off." Then Rick continued the search for his cell phone. Scratching his head, he said, "Call my number," and when Kevin did they heard only the ring from his receiver.

"I must have left it in the car," he murmured before heading downstairs to the garage.

And when he reached the bottom of the stairs and opened the side door, he found himself standing in an empty room.

Kevin came up behind him and stated the obvious. "Your car's not here."

That explained where his keys were, and since he was now sure he'd tossed them on the coffee table next to his cell phone, he knew it was gone, too.

"I take it you didn't lend it to your lady friend," Kevin said.

"Not voluntarily."

A sour taste hit Rick's tongue and it wasn't the bad coffee. Upstairs they began searching his house, looking for anything else missing and checking the doors and windows for signs of entry.

"You always leave your back door unlocked?" Kevin called from the kitchen.

"Never."

"Well, someone did." Kevin stepped into the living room, his face grim and sympathetic. "What about everything else? Your wallet, any valuables?"

"My wallet's in the bedroom. It wasn't touched."

"So someone just wanted your car and your phone."

"Looks like it," Rick said, easing down on the couch and rubbing his face in his hands. He tried to consider an explanation, one that didn't involve him being screwed over by a cunning redhead.

It wasn't looking good.

As if Kevin had read his thoughts, he asked, "How well do you know your lady friend?"

Rick snorted. There were a number of things he knew intimately about Jessica Beane—if that was her real name. He knew about the freckle southwest of her navel, that she shuddered when he kissed the backs of her knees, and that when she came, her cheeks flushed into pale pink circles. He knew she had a talented tongue and even more talented fingers, and that when he hit a sensitive spot, she purred like a kitten.

But did he know if she was a car thief? Whether their entire evening together wasn't just a long, drawn-out plot to rob him while he slept? That was anyone's guess.

He dug his fingers through his hair. "Apparently not well enough. I'm not sure she stole the car, but she was gone by the time I woke up."

He felt like an idiot just saying it out loud, and as his situation began to sink in, a coil of anger curled in his gut.

Kevin sighed. "Let me go get my pad and we'll start making notes."

"We've got bigger problems than a stolen car."

That stopped Kevin in his tracks, and when he spotted the look in Rick's eyes, his shoulders slumped. "No. Tell me the laptop wasn't in the car."

"The trunk."

"Thornton's lawyers will have a field day with this. It was gonna be bad enough telling them we're still holding the laptop after they got the judge to release it." Leaning a hand against the wall, he shook his head. "You're in for one hell of an ass chewing."

Rick really didn't give a squat about Thornton's lawyers or the raking he'd get from their department. That laptop had been his one hope at finding something on Creed. Hell, it was more than hope. Rick had been certain that his computer friend would get something off that machine, which would finally get them a solid lead.

And now it was gone.

A cold curtain of fury came over him, tightening his lip and clenching his fists at his sides. "I need to get it back," he stated. "It's as simple as that."

"I'll call in an APB on the vehicle. Maybe we'll get lucky."

Rising from the couch, Rick took determined steps to his bedroom and flipped on the shower. "While you're doing that, get what you can on a Jessica Beane. That's Beane with an E." He tried to remember the name of her store and only recalled she'd said it was on Powell. Had that been a lie? Was there truth in anything she'd said last night?

The thought that he'd been duped stung in more ways than he cared to analyze, and as he tossed off his jeans and headed for the bathroom, he chose to stay focused on the task at hand instead.

"Give me a minute. I'll need a ride to the station," he called out.

"You'll need more than a ride to the station."

Kevin had said it as a joke, but it was true. Today he'd need something he hadn't had in a long time—a lucky break. And without a doubt, the place to start was by finding one brassy Texas redhead.

The only question was, what would he do when he found her?

4

"GEORGIA, I'm so sorry."

It was the umpteenth time Jessie had made the statement since running home that morning and confirming her worst fears.

It was true. Wade had been in their apartment. And though barely a sock had been upturned in their dresser drawers, everything she and Georgia had of value was gone.

Granna Hawley's jewelry, Grandpa Hawley's watch. Her ruby-studded class ring from Tulouse High and the diamond-chip necklace she'd gotten for Christmas from Treat Wayans, her first boyfriend from the eighth grade.

Jessie's black velvet stash box had been emptied, Georgia's kitschy pink piggy bank drained. But worst of all was the fate of her and Georgia's most cherished possessions. Georgia's was her mother's diamond ring and Jessie's was the army commendation medal that belonged to the father she barely remembered.

Her granna Hawley had given it to her on her sixteenth birthday, handed over with words Jessie would never forget. "This is the stock you came from," Granna said, gripping the medal tightly in Jessie's hand. "Your mother may have changed your name, but you're still a Hawley through and through. And Hawleys are winners."

She'd handed Jessie the medal, telling her to think of her dead father, to take it as a reminder of what she was capable of and to never lose sight of the proud blood that ran through her veins.

Jessie had taken it, then turned around and married Wade Griggs, criminal extraordinaire.

How was that for a Hawley winner?

"It's not your fault," Georgia replied, also for the umpteenth time. And though Jessie tried to believe it, she couldn't reconcile Georgia's words with the solemn look of pain in her eyes. Just like Jessie's medal, that diamond ring meant everything to Georgia. It was one of the few things left from Georgia's mother who had died when Georgia was a teen. It had been that common ground, the loss of a parent, that brought Jessie and Georgia together as friends back in high school. And no one knew better than Jessie how much the ring meant.

"I'll get it back," Jessie promised. "If I have to scour every pawnshop in the country, I'm getting it back."

Georgia's smile was shrouded in doubt, and the truth made Jessie's heart bleed. Though neither wanted to say it, they both knew the rotten odds of ever seeing their possessions again. It would take a miracle, and miracles didn't come by Jessie often—if ever at all.

"Did you call your lawyer back home?" Georgia asked, opting to focus on something that still held a ray of promise.

"He's closed for the weekend. I left a message."

She tried to hide the sense of doom from her voice, but feared she was doing a sorry job of it. As if losing their valuables wasn't bad enough, Jessie had found the manila envelope she'd remembered so vividly. The one she'd been certain contained the signed copies of her divorce papers.

And breathing a long sigh of relief, she'd opened the metal clip and pulled out the contents, gratified there was at least one thing she could stop worrying about.

But the envelope didn't contain any divorce papers. It contained her granna's will.

Jessie had torn apart her black plastic file box and everything else in their apartment, searching through every last shred of paper she'd saved over the years. She'd found the divorce papers, all right. But they hadn't been signed by her or Wade. It had only been the copy she'd made before the documents were signed.

How she could have made such a mistake astounded her to the point of disbelief. And now, her only hope rested on the lawyer she'd retained. Surely his office would have a signed copy, and at least the matter of her divorce would end up no more than a temporary scare.

Georgia sprayed cleaner over a glass display case in their shop, Hidden Gems, and wiped the surface clean. Jessie and Georgia were among six artists who owned and operated the store, each offering their personal specialty in apparel and accessories.

Jessie sold her Beane Bags and Georgia made hand-painted silk scarves. Swan was an artisan in Native American, Aztec and Mexican jewelry, and Sonora had an eye for the latest trend in antique baubles. Candace made hats and Vickey constructed all kinds of wraps and jackets with her panels of exotic faux fur.

Among the six, Hidden Gems had recently gained notoriety in upscale fashion accessories, Jessie's latest nod by Hollywood bringing them all a welcomed slice of attention. And though today wasn't Jessie and Georgia's day to mind the shop, the recent influx in business brought them down to help keep things clean and in order.

"I'm sure Roger will have a copy of those divorce papers for you when he gets in on Monday," Georgia said, carefully placing a collection of Sonora's antique Bakelite jewelry back on the shelf.

"I hope you're right," Jessie said, the thought throwing another pit into the rocky bowels of her stomach.

She took a breath and tried to squelch it like she always did.

A magnet for misfortune, Jessie had learned years ago that busy hands made for clear minds. It was how she'd stumbled into the craft of making beaded purses in the first place. When her stepbrothers caught her up in their mischief or her stepfather's schemes landed the family back in poverty, Jessie would hole up in her room, stringing beads and sewing sequins. For hours on end, she'd ignore the screaming matches going on outside her door by losing herself in the ornate patterns she'd create.

She'd use beads when she had the money, any material she could find when she didn't. With as little as a roll of fishing line and a bag of screw-top soda caps, she'd learned to string bags and accessories out of anything she could tap a hole through. She'd loved the peace the tedious task brought to her often chaotic childhood. And to this day, when the world seemed to swallow her up, she strung beads to see it through.

Georgia sighed. "They'll have those papers. Don't you worry."

But worry was all Jessie had left. As she looked around the store, she wondered how she'd be able to keep her partnership here if Wade had a right to half her income.

None of this was cheap, and she was plum out of credit. She'd already extended herself to the hilt to pay rent in the city, and she knew as well as anyone that Hollywood trends left as fast as they came. She'd needed this windfall to get ahead and create a nest egg so she could reinvent herself once Beane Bags became yesterday's news.

If Wade was entitled to half of it—

She gritted her teeth and shoved away the thought. Brushing a black felt hat with an added dose of swiftness, she considered all the things she'd do before she let that happen.

She'd burn her inventory and declare bankruptcy before she let Wade Griggs take another dime from her. And come Monday, she'd get in touch with the lawyer who would confirm her divorce and put all her worries at ease.

That would leave her only with the insurmountable task of trying to recover her and Georgia's most sacred keepsake.

That familiar nausea broke through the anger and settled back in her stomach. They'd filled out a police report this morning, but even the patrolman who answered the call told them the chance of recovering their things was all but none. Wade had come in from out of state, and only if he were stupid enough to try to pawn the items anywhere near San Francisco would they have the slimmest opportunity to getting anything back.

She needed to know where he'd gone. She needed to somehow trace his steps since yesterday evening. In short, she needed one of those elusive miracles she never seemed to come across.

Or maybe a hero.

And as if that thought had been a summons, she looked up to catch the ring of the door and the sight of the one man who might qualify for the job.

Inspector Rick Marshall.

Straightening her stance, she felt a little flip in her chest at the vision of the only good thing that had happened to her in the last twenty-four hours. And oh, had he been good. Right now, she'd give anything to be in his bed, his hard body and her soft moves creating a symphony of orgasmic delight. It jumped her pulse just thinking about it as he snaked through the displays toward her.

Silhouetted against the sharp sunlight, he looked broader and more muscular than he had the night before, his calm, measured steps expressing that familiar, cool confidence that had attracted her at the bar. He wore a dark suit jacket in spite of the August heat. Coupled with the po-larized Ray-Bans, he looked like Secret Service, or maybe FBI, that slick, dark hair, sharp, pointed nose and rigid jaw polishing off what should be the poster child for sexy, steel-bodied law enforcement.

She wondered if he had a weapon holstered under one arm. Something big and dangerous, like a shiny .44 Magnum or a dark, steely Glock.

The thought ramped up her heartbeat. She'd always had a thing for a man in uniform, and though her gut still hung heavy with worry, her mouth curved in a hopeful smile. Maybe Rick had caught wind of the police report they'd filed and had come to see if she was okay. Or maybe their encounter last night had him coming back for seconds. Either option would be a ray of sunshine on this bleary day.

"Well, if it isn't SFPD's finest," she quipped, marvel-ing over those firm set lips and the perpetual furrow in his brow. He looked so serious, like a man on a mission, and she wondered which playful move might soften those hard lines into a smile.

She had a few in her arsenal—a couple already proven successful.

But as he drew closer and pulled off his shades, she saw the ire in his eyes. He wasn't as pleased to see her as she was him, and she quickly surmised that in her panic last night, she probably should have stopped to leave a quick note. He clearly wasn't happy, and when he stopped to loom ominously over her, she flattened her smile and cleared her throat.

"Look, Sheriff, about last night—"

"I'm not a sheriff," he said, hardly moving his lips.

Oh, yeah. He was angry, all right, and the cause of her quick pulse shifted from lust to annoyance.

For criminy sakes, he'd made it clear right from the start. Last night was a one-time thing. Two ships passing in the night. No expectations, no hard feelings. So the fact that he'd tracked her down simply because she hadn't kissed him goodbye seemed pretty absurd.

"Fine, Inspector Marshall, then," she said, gripping a hand to her hip and jutting up her chin.

She silently huffed. Oh, she *so* did not need this, nor did she feel obligated to explain. But having her fill of problems for one day, she offered an apology anyway.

"Look, I'm sorry for ducking out on you like that. I—"

"I just want my car back."

His teeth were clenched tight. Those damning blue eyes bore holes through her thoughts and his words tripped her back a step.

"What?"

He stepped closer and lowered his voice. "Tell me where I can find my car and we'll forget the whole thing happened, *Ms. Beane.*" Then glancing sideways toward Georgia, he added, "Or should I say, *Mrs. Griggs.*"

Jessie's jaw dropped and Georgia stepped up to her side.

"She's not Mrs. Griggs," Georgia defended.

He flashed her friend a cool stare. "No? I've got a number of aliases to choose from. How about Sugar Jessica Hawley? Jessica Griggs? Or my favorite, Sugar Beane?"

Jessie gaped. "You looked me up?"

"I pulled your prints from my bedpost."

Heat ran up her cheeks, only half of it from the memory of how those prints ended up on his bedpost. But as this scene began to sink in, she chose to focus on the half that came from being royally ticked off.

"How dare you!"

Georgia wedged a shoulder between Jessie and Rick, stepping in as Jessie's protector as she'd been doing for the past decade. "Do you run rap sheets on all the women you sleep with?"

"Only the ones who steal my car."

Jessie pushed in front of Georgia, nearly toppling over Candace's display of felt and feather hats, to press her nose close to Rick's chest.

He was taller than she'd recalled, too, but she hadn't let things like that intimidate her yet.

"I don't know what you're talking about."

"Then let me refresh your memory." His frown deepened and those stormy eyes turned dark as rain clouds. "My car was stolen, and the last woman I saw it with has a long list of criminal charges starting with grand theft auto and conspiracy to commit fraud."

"Every one of those charges against me was dropped."

"Maybe the Colbrook County police need to reopen their files."

Jessie gasped, not knowing whether to spit or cry.

Ever since she rolled out of this man's bed twelve hours ago her life had gone from top of the hill to bottomless hell, and it seemed to be sinking farther. It was bad enough she was about to lose everything she'd worked hard for over the last year, *now she was being accused of a crime?*

Then a dark sense of familiarity washed through her, shoving her from a state of shock into the reality of the situation.

Oh, she'd been here before. She'd stood right in front of the law and had the same accusations thrown at her almost two years ago. Back then, she'd been ignorant and stupid, her innocence working against her and costing her everything she had.

She was smarter now.

This whole scene had Wade Griggs written all over it, and having charted these waters before, she knew exactly which mistakes she would not repeat.

Crossing her arms over her chest, she threw her shoulders back and stood firm. "If you're accusing me of a crime, I demand to see a lawyer."

"Yeah," Georgia echoed, but their partner, Swan, didn't seem to be thrilled with the idea of a fight.

She stepped out from the main counter, rushing over to the three of them while a dozen bangle bracelets sounded like wind chimes around her wrists. Flashing a forced and nervous smile, she cocked her head toward a small group of customers perusing Georgia's scarves.

"Excuse me," Swan said in her most pleasant and patronizing tone. "This sounds like a conversation that needs to be taken in the back." Then lowering her voice to below a whisper, she added, "Our customers are getting curious."

Rick placed a hand on Jessie's arm and replied, "I have a better idea. We'll take this down to the station."

Every part of Jessie wanted to kick him in the shins and scream bloody murder. This was just like last time. Accuse first, ask questions later. But in this case, it was worse. This time, she'd opened a soft spot for her accuser. She'd shared a blissful and passionate evening with a man she'd thought was gentle and kind.

Sure, they hadn't gone through old scrapbooks and swapped schoolyard memories, but they'd connected on a level more intuitive than that. Maybe it had only been a one-night stand, but the fact that her lover could be so warm and intimate one minute then turn on her the next stung deep and hard, and the fighter in her wanted to open a wound in return.

But Swan was right. Even the look in Georgia's eyes echoed that. This was their business, the livelihood that supported them all, and creating a scene in the middle of it wouldn't do anyone any good. Jessie had enough troubles. She didn't need to add five angry partners wanting to throw her out of the co-op. So swallowing her hurt and pride, she jerked her hand from his grasp and stepped toward the counter where she'd left her purse.

"Of course," she said, using a haughty tone that came out sounding like Miss Hathaway from the *Beverly Hillbillies*. Raising her voice so the customers could hear clearly, she added, "I'm sure Mr. Marshall and I can straighten out this matter over coffee."

Grabbing the orange Beane Bag that she only now remembered still held her green lacy bra from the night before, she took clipped steps to the double glass doors. Holding her head high and her mouth shut, they'd moved down the street well past the eyes and ears of Hidden Gems.

Then she turned on her heels and jabbed a finger into his chest. "If you ever come into my place of business and embarrass me like that again, I promise you'll rue the day you met me."

He clasped her forearm and steered her across the street. "I already do."

Now that was just cruel, and a mix of hurt, frustration and anger erupted in a sting of tears at the backs of her eyes. Was she a magnet for jerks? Back home, she'd blamed youth and ignorance for the mistakes she'd made. That and the fact that her stepbrothers usually chased the good guys away. But she was in California now, away from the influence of her family and wiser than her years. So why was it the first man she'd opened herself up to could be as bad as all the rest?

"Then I'll find a way to make it worse," she muttered, part in frustration, part in vengeance. How many more knocks could she take today before she finally split in two?

"You do that," he said. "But in the meantime, you're going to tell me where the hell I can find my car."

"I told you, I don't know what you're talking about."

"We'll see about that."

He led her up to a silver sedan then stopped at the passenger side door. She noted it wasn't a typical squad car. There were no lights, no caged backseat with the interior door handles missing and bulletproof glass to protect the driver from hardened criminals like herself who might come at them with an emery board.

Jerking her arm from his grasp, she stepped close to his chest, trying to ignore that familiar rugged scent that had her hot and bothered the night before. Her forehead just reached the tip of his chin and the memory of her lips closing over that smoothly shaven throat left her mouth dry.

She stiffened her bottom lip and spat out, "Aren't you going to cuff me?"

The slight quirk of his brow said more than he'd ever admit. Maybe he wasn't completely immune to the night they'd shared. But as quickly as it flashed by, the set jaw returned and the stony cop was back.

"Do I need to?" he asked.

She tried not to be sarcastic and sour, her smarter side recognizing that honey went a lot further than spite.

The smarter side lost. She was too mad.

"According to you? Probably. You seem to think I'm capable of all kinds of heinous acts."

He opened the door and offered a hand. "I'll take my chances."

She slapped it off and climbed into the passenger seat, wincing when he slammed the door and rounded the car to take the seat next to her.

This was officially her second escorted trip downtown in as many years. Her first ride had been to the Colbrook County jail and was the opening scene to a nightmare that became twelve of the most rotten months of her life.

Would this trip end up any better?

Glancing over at the ice block of a man sitting next to her, she couldn't help but fear the worst.

5

RICK PULLED AWAY from the curb and headed south on Powell toward his office at the Hall of Justice. There was an extra edge to his already agitated state thanks to his unexpected reaction to seeing Jessie again. He thought he'd worked up enough fury over what had happened to erase all the lusty remnants of the night they'd shared. But the moment he saw her standing there cute and casual, those strawberry curls haphazardly framing her face and those wet, rosy lips curved in a smile, every second of their sexual encounter sped through his mind on a course straight for his cock.

The rush of heat had tipped him off balance, swinging the scales in the wrong direction. He'd walked in with intimidation on his mind and walked out with a woman in his hands and too many wrong ideas in his head. And now, instead of planning his interrogation, he was gripping white knuckles to the steering wheel, trying to veer his thoughts off her sweet scent and those sexy bare legs.

Did the woman own a pair of jeans, or was her entire wardrobe geared to give him wood?

Her short skirt grazed around midthigh, and she wore it with a wide, beaded belt that hung low like a holster on her hips, accentuating her curves and trimming an already slim waist. A double-layered T-shirt finished off an outfit that was simple and flirty and sexy in one bundle. How was he supposed to focus with all that naked flesh and the memory of what she could do with it fighting for space in his thoughts?

Muttering a silent curse, he glanced over to see one angry Texas beauty. With her shoulders squared, her arms crossed over her chest and her nose firmly pointed toward the window, she looked like a rebellious teenager who'd just been grounded. Which made it all the more ludicrous that he couldn't shake his urge to drive her back to his bedroom where the whole mess started.

He tried to squelch it by focusing on the trouble she'd caused him, tossing in a dash of rage over what she might be hiding. It was only marginally successful.

"I didn't steal your car," she snapped.

"So you claim."

He turned down Post Street to avoid the cable cars on Powell only to get stuck behind a Lombardi's Bakery truck stopped to make a delivery. After a Beetle passed on his right, Rick darted around and headed down Stockton, intent on getting to the station and getting this over with as quickly as possible.

"I mean," she added, "if I had stolen your car, do you really think I'd be standing around in my shop later the same day?"

"I don't know. You tell me."

She turned and aimed a fiery scowl in his direction. "If you remember, *I* was the one who told you where I worked. Would a thief tell you where to find her? Do you really think that?"

So much for not talking without her lawyer.

He crossed Geary and headed toward O'Farrell, nearly running down a distracted shopper trying to cross the two-lane intersection on a red. He wondered how many pedestrians had to get killed in the city every year before people paid attention to traffic lights.

"I know what you're thinking." Now she was jabbing that slim finger at him like it was a tiny pickax. "You're thinking I was part of a setup."

"The thought crossed my mind."

She scoffed. "Don't you think that's a little extreme? That I spent the whole evening with you just so I could steal your—what was it—a Chrysler?"

"Dodge Charger."

She threw out an exasperated laugh. "You think I'd pick you up in a bar, go home to your place, strip my clothes off and have hours and hours of sex with you for a Dodge Charger?"

No, he didn't. Based on the evidence, his instincts and a long conversation with the Colbrook County sheriff's department, he'd all but concluded she hadn't stolen his car. But he wasn't ready to share that yet, nor let her off the hook for what she *had* done.

So he opted to keep letting her sweat. "I've seen stranger things."

She stared at him, her expression blank for a number of beats until it morphed into something he hadn't expected. "You could think that of me?" she asked, her voice shallow and small. "After everything we shared? After..." Tiny pools welled in her eyes and her chin began to quiver as her affronted glare gave way to a sharp stab of hurt.

Oh, crap. He'd overplayed his hand and was about to

get hit with waterworks. He hated tears. He could deal with anything but tears.

Speeding down Fourth, he quickly pulled into a fire zone and threw the car in Park. This encounter had started off wrong and was moving south with every second. It was time to pull it together.

"Okay, look." He tossed an arm over the seat to face her square in the eye. "I know you didn't steal my car, but you had something to do with it. And unless you want to be held responsible, you're going to come down to my office and tell me every move you made between the time I fell asleep last night and five minutes ago when I found you back there dusting hats."

She sat expressionless for a moment until his words sunk in, then slowly the furrow returned to her brow and her mouth dropped open.

"*You know* I didn't steal your car?"

He turned back to the steering wheel and grumbled, "The evidence doesn't support it."

"Yet you stormed into my place of business and accused me of being a thief in front of my partners and customers?"

Anger. Good. It was an emotion he could deal with, and it came with the extra bonus that it would keep her pitted against him in case he did something stupid like ask her back to his place later.

He shifted the car in gear and pulled back into traffic.

She gaped. "You humiliated me."

"I think that's a slight exaggeration."

"You treated me like a criminal."

"If I treated you like a criminal, I would have come with backup and you'd be in the backseat of a squad car sitting on handcuffs."

"You jerk!"

"Listen, sweetheart. You aren't innocent by a long shot. You've got a lot of explaining to do."

She snapped her mouth shut and returned to the grounded teenager pose, her defiant eyes staring straight ahead and her lips pressed taut as a tightrope. "You can talk to my lawyer."

That was beginning to sound like a *good* thing. Unfortunately, unless she had a lawyer who happened to be twiddling his thumbs at the moment and possibly sitting in the hallway outside Homicide, he didn't have the luxury of time. He'd already wasted a good portion of the day pulling strings to have fingerprints run, talking to Texas law enforcement—*who seemingly had all day to chat*—and piecing together what had gone down at his house while he'd slept. Now that he'd found Jessie, he needed her to put the final pieces together, and fast.

Swallowing his pride for the sake of his investigation, he offered, "I'm sorry. It's just so rare I get to throw my badge around and act all coplike."

Okay, not the best apology, but considering he preferred to keep her angry with him, it was the best he could do.

She glanced his way and in her eyes he thought he might have seen a slight break in the storm. Or maybe she was only calculating the many more ways she could stick it to him. He couldn't tell, because before he'd gotten a good look, she'd flipped her gaze back to the street ahead.

Damn, this woman was full of spit and fire. Which just made him want her more.

It was another stern reminder that he needed to get her statement, find out what she'd done last night then send her back to her purse shop. She'd caused him enough trouble for one lifetime, and his body's relentless urges to get her back in the sack only proved how strung out he'd become. He seriously needed a vacation. A long one. On a remote island filled with enough women and sex to right his tilted preferences where that was concerned.

He turned off Seventh and pulled up to the Hall of Justice, double-parking alongside an Acura before shutting off the engine.

"Come with me," he said, and this time she didn't argue. Instead she grabbed her purse and followed him up the steps and through the glass doors. They took the elevator to his floor then stepped down the long, tiled corridor. And as if his day couldn't get any worse, waiting for him near the door to Homicide were Paolo and Lucy Mendoza.

The short, dark-skinned man stood when he saw them coming while his wife remained seated, pressing an embroidered handkerchief to her wet, reddened nose. It was the way he usually found them ever since the day he'd shown up at their home to tell them their daughter was dead. Paolo always stood and did the talking, and Lucy sat and cried. Except now, four months later, Paolo looked older and wearier. Tired lines creased his brow, and the anger in his eyes had deteriorated to the dark emptiness of a man who knew he should let go but would never find the way.

Rick knew that feeling. Those were the eyes he saw in the mirror every morning.

"Inspector Marshall," Paolo said, despite the dozens of times he'd been asked to call him Rick. "The newspaper said Creed Thornton is no longer a suspect."

Rick stopped and shook his head. "That's not true. Everyone is still a suspect."

"They said you've released his possessions from

evidence. There was a picture of him smiling outside the courthouse, waving a hand like a free man. His lawyer said he'd been cleared."

Like Rick, Paolo was certain Creed Thornton killed his daughter, even though Rick had been careful never to specifically admit it.

He stepped between the couple, moving his hand from Paolo's shoulder to Lucy's. She responded by deepening her sobs, and it turned the crank on the vise around his gut.

He clenched his teeth and fought to keep his composure. "No one's been cleared, and not everything was returned. There are still some things we're looking at."

"What things?"

He shot a pained looked at both of them, wishing he could tell them everything but knowing he couldn't. "When I have something to tell, I will. Please, rest assured that neither Creed nor anyone else has been taken off the list of suspects. We're still working very hard to find out who murdered your daughter."

"They still say she killed herself," cried Lucy from behind her wet cloth.

He looked into Paolo's eyes, the raw emotion in them opening up wounds Rick felt would never heal.

"I'm not giving up," was all he could say. And after the two men shared a glance that said more than words, Paolo reached for his wife and motioned for them to go, nodding his acceptance over what he'd been told.

"You're a good man, Inspector Marshall. You say you'll catch the killer, I believe you."

Feeling as though the life had just been sucked out of him, Rick simply nodded and watched as they shuffled down the hall and out of sight.

"Those poor people," Jessie whispered. "What happened to their daughter?"

"That's what I was about to find out before my car was stolen."

Jessie shook her head. "I don't understand."

Stepping back to the door, he muttered, "Never mind."

The encounter had brought him directly to what this meeting with Jessie was about. What his *life* was about. And to that end, he was thankful the Mendozas had chosen this moment to pay a visit. Like a sign from above, he'd needed the reminder that there were more important things in life than dark, sexy nights and fiery-hot redheads. There were people in real pain that needed him to stay clear and focused so that maybe, unlike him, they could find closure to their tragedy. And somewhere in there, maybe he could close enough tragedies to finally bring peace to his own.

He guided her through the door and into the offices of Homicide, interested heads turning as the two made their way to one of the conference rooms near the back. It looked as if word of his evening had gotten around. A number of mouths curved into smiles, but every one of the officers in the unit was smart enough to keep their mouth shut.

All except for Agent Hurley, a former police chief's son with more guts than brains.

"Not bad, Marshall," Hurley said, nodding an approval as he gave Jessie the once-over.

It was the move that nearly snapped his composure. Between an investigation shot to hell and a one-night-stand that left him more frustrated than satisfied, he'd welcome the chance to blow off steam. Turning a steely glare to the lanky youth, he pondered just how good it would feel to plant a couple of fists in that jaw and batter that cocky smile off his face. And he said as much with a glance and a twitch in his hand.

It was enough to back even Hurley down.

6

JESSIE FOLLOWED Rick through a maze of desks and cubicles as they made their way toward the offices along the back wall. Though her ride downtown had felt as familiar as her last arrest, San Francisco's Hall of Justice was a far cry from the one-story brick building that housed the Colbrook County sheriff's department. With its long, quiet corridors, marble walls and numbered office doors, this building looked more like a state capitol than a courthouse and police station, and the stateliness of it left Jessie feeling very small.

It was only when they'd entered Rick's offices that she'd regained some semblance of control, the murmur of conversation and the buzz of ringing phones bringing back a casual air of regular people doing regular jobs.

Rick held a light hand to her shoulder as they crossed the room, and the collection of glances they gathered along the way contained more than casual curiosity. They must all know about last night, and Jessie suspected that in the microclimate of San Francisco's Homicide Unit, the big city might not be all that different from Tulouse, Texas.

"What did he mean?" she asked when they stepped out of earshot of the tall cop who had just proverbially undressed her with his lewd smile.

"Agent Wiseguy is perfecting his comedy routine," Rick replied. "It still needs work." He said it loud enough to elicit some nearby chuckles and she tried to let the laughter settle her nerves. But between the courtly building and the heart-ripping eyes of that couple in the hall, she doubted she'd ease. At least not until she got out of this place and stepped back onto the busy street.

If Rick had brought her here in the hope of intimidating her, it was working. Right now, the only thing she cared to do was tell him what he wanted and get the hell out.

And when he led her into a small conference room and closed the door behind them, that's exactly what she did.

From the ring of her phone when Georgia had called the night before to the moment she'd dashed into the back of the yellow cab, Jessie recounted her every step. She didn't miss the tiniest detail while he listened to her story and paced the small room. And when she was done, she felt an odd sense of relief, as if somehow thanks to her confession this tall, dark-haired cop might be able to fix everything for her. She hadn't realized it, but in the process of explaining the events of the last twelve hours, a seed of hope had sprouted in her spirit. Like maybe Rick could find Wade, and Georgia's diamond ring, and her father's army medal.

Yeah, and in the glove compartment of his stolen Dodge Charger they'd find her signed divorce papers. Or maybe he'd have a time machine that could transport her back twenty-four hours, or a month, or a year, or better yet, back before the day she'd looked into Wade Griggs's eyes and uttered, "I do."

She huffed to herself, acknowledging that the thought was as ridiculous as the hope she'd manifested. Because studying Rick's expression, she could clearly see she wasn't the one he was interested in saving. And when it came to men in general, she wondered how old she'd have to be before she stopped believing in that particular fairy tale.

"So let me make sure I understand this." Rick's voice was slow and deliberate as he stopped pacing and stood ominously before her. "Your husband—"

"*Ex*-husband."

"—is released from jail, crosses three state lines in violation of his parole, threatens and harasses you while standing out on the street—" Then he paused and pinched the bridge of his nose between his thumb and forefinger. "And not once did you consider waking up the *police officer* sleeping in the room next to you?"

"I actually did," she said, her voice quiet but matter-of-fact.

"Instead, you fled, leaving both the front and back doors unlocked because…"

The anger in his voice squeezed her insides.

She swallowed, trying to decide how far back in her lifetime she needed to go to convey the fact that not once had anyone besides her grandmother ever come to her rescue. That no matter how many times her knee-jerk reaction was to believe someone might defend her, her good senses always won over, reminding her that in her life, Jessica Beane could only fully count on Jessica Beane.

Oh, sure, her mother had stood up for her on occasion, which usually spurred some sort of fight at home. But whenever a choice had to be made between her daughter and her new husband, Jessie always drew the short straw. The trend started at home and spanned throughout practically every relationship she'd had. So assuming things would be different with a man she'd only just met was too much of a stretch even for her optimistic nature.

But she decided to skip the history. "I didn't want to involve you in my problems."

He exhaled a sharp breath and opened his mouth to spout something, but she was spared the lecture by the entrance of a short Asian man.

"We got a lead on your cell phone," the man said.

The scalding look in Rick's eyes lightened.

"It was used about an hour ago to call a number in Reno, Nevada. I looked it up. It's a pawnshop right on the main drag."

Jessie's stomach did a flip. "Do you mean Wade? Did Wade call a pawnshop?"

The man looked at Jessie without saying a word, his expression neither confirming nor denying her assumption.

She rose from the chair. "Is that Wade?" she asked again, this time with more urgency. If Wade had called a pawnshop, that meant she could track her things down and make at least some of this right.

Rick ignored her and turned to the man. "Did you call the Reno police?"

"They've put an APB on your car, but they've all but promised no one will be looking for it. They're in the middle of Hot August Nights. They've got over a quarter million people in town for the event and more action than they can deal with at the moment." He thumbed through a small pad of paper and examined his notes. "They said it will be well after next week before the town is cleared and life gets back to normal." Then he glanced at Rick and sighed. "I guess your guy found the perfect place to disappear."

Rick's eyes darkened, but it was the only sign of disappointment on his face. "Any idea where he was when he called?"

The man shook his head. "No, they weren't able to triangulate and the call didn't last long enough. They only gave me the number he called, but I think it's a good guess your car thief is either in Reno or he's on his way."

"You *are* talking about Wade," she said, stepping closer to the two men. "What pawnshop did he call?"

"Jess, it's a police matter," Rick attempted, but given this was the first good news she'd heard all day, she wasn't having any of it.

"Like hell it is. I need to get my jewelry back. You know he's called a pawnshop to cash in on the jewelry he stole."

She tried to temper her excitement. If she could return Georgia's ring to her, at least one person in the mix would walk away with nothing lost. And of all the people involved, Georgia was the one she cared about most. Rick had only lost a car, one his insurance company would surely replace. And Jessie…well, she was used to losing the things she cared about.

But if she could spare Georgia…

"We'll look into retrieving your things," Rick said, holding up a hand.

His patronizing tone lit a fire between her temples. How many times had she heard promises like that before? She knew damn well tracking down the items Wade stole from her apartment would be low on their priority list, and that if she wanted them back, she'd have to go get them herself.

Rushing to the table, she grabbed her purse and turned. "I've told you everything about last night. Now I need to go." Then she moved toward the door, not interested in waiting for an answer. They wouldn't tell her where Wade called, but the man said it was Reno and on the main drag—wherever that was. It was enough information to get her started, for sure.

She crossed the room, but was halted when Rick snapped a firm hand to her arm.

"You aren't going anywhere."

"Watch me."

His grip tightened and so did his lips. "Sit down, Jess."

She narrowed her eyes and stood straight, hoping to close the distance between her height and his. She'd spent enough time in police stations lately to know exactly what these two cops were *not* going to do for her. If she was on her own, there'd be no time wasted. "Are you charging me with a crime?"

"You know the answer to that."

"Then let me go. We're done here."

She attempted to pull her arm away, but he held on tighter, now nearly to the point of pain.

"You're not chasing off to Reno."

"Oh, yes, I am." She eyed him and then his coworker. "You heard the man. Reno's in the middle of Hot Nights, or whatever they call it. And if you think I'm waiting forever for you and your red tape to get my things back, you're sorely mistaken."

He gripped his hands to her shoulders and shoved her down into a nearby chair. "Then I'll hold you for obstruction of justice."

"What justice? You aren't interested in what Wade stole from me and Georgia. You only want your car back."

The two men shared a glance, causing Rick to soften his glare. "How did you leave things with Reno PD?"

The man shrugged. "Like I said, not much they can do. Hot August Nights is a big event. Lots of extra people in town and they're up to their ears in thefts, drunken brawls and robberies." He tilted his head toward Jessie. "If you want to get anything back, including the vehicle, you are pretty much on your own, at least for a couple weeks."

"I don't have that long," Rick mumbled, and Jessie began to wonder if there was more to this than his car.

What was the hurry for him? All he had to do was file a claim with his insurance and he'd have a check in his hand to go buy something shiny and new.

Did he owe more on it than it was worth? He didn't strike her as a man hurting for money. Though his house in the Sunset was modest and sparsely decorated, the furnishings hadn't been cheap. Jess wasn't an expert on interiors, but she knew budget furniture when she saw it and Rick's house hadn't fit the bill. He may not be a millionaire, but she knew the man wasn't strapped for cash. So why the frantic search for a car he could easily replace?

The coworker flashed a look of apology. "I've got court in the morning. The Claussen case. I can't miss it."

"I'll take this myself," Rick said, and Jessie rose.

"You're going after Wade?"

He shot her an angry glare. "You stay put."

"I'm going with you."

"You're going back to your shop on Powell."

"Like hell. I'm going to Reno to get Georgia's ring."

"You'll do what I say or I'll have you thrown in a holding cell for the next three days."

They stared each other down. She didn't have to be a psychologist to see this conversation wasn't going anywhere, so she decided to redirect.

Holding her purse to her side, she smiled pleasantly. "You're right. I'll go back to my shop on Powell." Then she took two steps toward the door. "You'll give me a call when you find something out?"

The Asian man glanced at Rick then made a move for the door. "I'll leave this to you," he called to Rick over his shoulder. Then he closed the door behind him before Jessie could grab the knob.

"You're not going after Wade."

She turned and widened her smile, trying to keep the truth from showing on her face. "Of course not. I don't want to get arrested. I'll just go back to work. You let me know when you hear something." Then she dug a business card out of her purse and handed it to him. "Here's my number."

"I'm not an idiot."

Neither was she, but instead of responding, she spun on her heels and opened the door.

His big hand shoved it closed.

Facing him, she noted the look in those sexy baby blues. He knew exactly what she was planning, but she'd stumped him by not arguing. And now he stood there trying to contemplate his next move, knowing damn well she was going to do what she pleased no matter what he said.

She tried to hold back a smirk. "Was there something else?"

He moved in, backing her up against the door and bracing his strong arm over her shoulder. His permanent scowl softened, and for the first time that day, he showed a sliver of resemblance to the sexy, playful man she'd gone home with last night.

She'd liked that version of him. Liked the way he was looking at her right now. Assessing. Calculating. His expression a mix of danger, promise and warning. It was a cop look, one he'd probably taken years to master, and he'd mastered it well. But focused on her it came with a sexual undertone that gave him an extra card in his pocket. It was a meticulously practiced survey intended to turn a witness on her side, to create fluster and confusion so the truth would leak through.

And Jessie had to admit, it was working.

For the longest time he simply stood close, studying her, processing her every breath, taking in each blink and flinch she made. Then those searing eyes lowered to her lips and his own lips twitched in response, as if he were considering bending down and taking a taste. A wave of heat rushed from her feet to the tips of her ears, flushing warmth to her cheeks and moistening the spot between her thighs.

Amazing. How could one look—one seductively threatening look—turn her from perturbed to desperately horny in the twist of a second?

He dipped his head and licked his lips, and her fingers curled against the hardwood door. God help her, she wanted him to kiss her. She ached for it. All from one steely look, and as she swallowed and tried to emerge from the lust, she felt the need to say something. Unfortunately she couldn't recall what they were talking about.

His pursed brow returned, and he spoke low and soft. Almost a whisper. "I guess I'm going to have to keep an eye on you, then."

An eye and several other body parts would be good.

He lifted his gaze back to hers. "You can ride along, but you'll do what I say, or so help me, I'll throw you on the first Greyhound back to the Bay Area."

Do what he said? He made it sound as if she'd be his slave. And with his mouth inches from hers, and her heart playing a drumbeat in her ears, the suggestion stirred up a number of fantasies, all involving highly erotic domination.

And Rick had handcuffs.

She blinked. What the hell were they talking about?

"Are we clear?" he asked.

Clear as mud. But when he straightened and she slid away, it all came back to her. Wade. They'd been talking about Wade. And if she wasn't mistaken, Rick had just agreed to let her go with him to Reno.

She nodded, her motor skills still not recovered enough to form words, and he responded by grabbing the knob and opening the door.

"Then after you," he said, holding out a hand.

And on legs the strength of oatmeal, she walked out of the office, wondering what exactly she'd agreed to.

7

Now, this was a move that had *bad idea* stamped all over it in big block letters. In fact, Rick could only think of one thing dumber than letting Jessie ride along in his search for Wade, and that was setting her loose to go looking for the man on her own. Given what he was learning of the brassy redhead, only two things would have come of that option. She'd either botch his efforts entirely or land herself in a mess of trouble—most likely accomplishing both in one shot.

So instead, here he was, an hour out of San Francisco, trying to figure out how she'd maneuvered an invite and, more importantly, how she'd managed to turn his life upside down in less than twenty-four hours.

He should be sitting in a dank apartment in the Haight, watching his Red Bull-chugging computer geek find the lead that would help him catch a murderer. He wasn't supposed to be traipsing off to Reno looking for a car thief.

And in light of everything she'd put him through, he *really* wasn't supposed to be wishing like the devil he could get back in Jessie Beane's pants.

Shifting in his seat, he tugged on his inseam, trying to make room in slacks that always seemed to tighten around her. As much as he tried, he couldn't wipe away the memory of the night they shared, and it wasn't helping having her inches away, taunting him with all that cleavage and those lush, sexy lips. How he was supposed to ignore her all night he had no idea, but sometime between now and Reno he'd need to learn. Because spending another night in bed with Jessica Beane was out of the question.

It was one thing to bring home a woman he never expected to see again. It was entirely different to come back for seconds. In Rick's book, anything past a one-night stand officially constituted dating, and that was a ritual he'd put on indefinite hold. He'd already tried it before, nearly a year after his wife's death, and all it had gotten him was hurt feelings and the painful reminder that he hadn't been ready to move on. And the months since then hadn't changed a thing.

If he'd learned anything in the last year, it was that wounded hearts made lousy lovers, and the sexy young woman beside him had already had her share of lousy lovers. She didn't need another notch in that particular bedpost. Which meant Rick needed to ice himself down and take orders from the head on his shoulders instead of the one in his pants.

He glanced at the time. It was six o'clock in the evening and they were still three hours from Reno. Unless they got lucky and found his Dodge parked outside the pawnshop with his laptop and Jessie's valuables inside, this was going to be a late night. Late enough that they'd most likely be looking for a hotel room.

A hotel room in Reno, *The Biggest Little City In The World.* A place full of food and drink and gambling. And temptation.

He flicked a finger to the switch and lowered his window an inch or two, hoping to suck her sweet, fruity scent from the air. It was the same one embedded in his sheets and still lingering on his fingers from the night before. The one he'd woken up enveloped in this morning when he'd reached out to pick up where they'd left off.

Unfinished business you could finish tonight, Ricky boy.

Oh, no, the last thing he needed was the little voice of unreason suggesting yet another BAD IDEA, and in an attempt to drown it out, he reached for the stereo.

"I'm not supposed to be here, you know."

He frowned and eyed Jessie. It was the first comment she'd made since they passed Fairfield twenty minutes ago.

"Yeah?" he grumbled. "Maybe you could have decided that before we left San Francisco."

With her nose pointed straight ahead, she fidgeted with the beads on her necklace. Her teeth held a clamp on that rosy bottom lip, and at some point since the last time he'd glanced over, she'd snapped her knees together prim and proper.

Ignoring his sarcasm, she replied, "It's against the rules."

"What rules?"

"Georgia's rules." And when she turned to meet his eyes, he saw something that looked like trepidation. "I wasn't supposed to see you again after last night."

"Would you mind telling me who Georgia is and who made her the keeper of your whereabouts?"

Not that he was arguing with the idea. His initial reaction was an instant affinity for Georgia, whoever she was.

"My roommate. My best friend. You met her last night, and again at the shop today." And with a look that said *duh*, she added, "The one I called right as we were leaving the city?"

"I wasn't paying attention," he admitted, though he kept to himself that it was because she'd chosen that moment to slip off her shoes and expose ten dainty little toes he'd gotten to know pretty well last night. In fact, the sight had brought back so many memories he'd nearly driven straight past the on-ramp to the Bay Bridge.

"The short brunette with the big hair and bigger hoop earrings?" she offered.

He nodded. "I remember. She has a thing for bright red lipstick."

Jessie moved the fidgeting from her necklace to the thin strap of her beaded purse. "You see, after Wade and a couple of crappy boyfriends before him, Georgia took over my love life. She said I needed to start focusing on me, to give the relationship thing a break and get in touch with the kind of man I want to be with, instead of taking the first guy who happens to be available. She's been coaching me. Wouldn't even let me think about men until I'd gotten my business off the ground and settled here in California."

"You've let your girlfriend keep you from dating?"

She shot him a sideways glance. "Georgia isn't easy to argue with. Besides, she knows what I've been through. I came here looking for help and she doesn't do anything halfway. So in addition to helping me get set up at the shop and kicking her roommate out so I could move in, I gave her full rein on my love life."

"She gave you rules."

That familiar affront returned to her eyes. "It's not like I have a stone tablet at the end of my bed."

He responded by raising a brow.

She huffed and turned her nose back to the dash. "Yes, she gave me rules. And rule number one is aimed at breaking the connection between sex and love."

"The one-night stand."

She shrugged. "I have to admit that was some of the best

sex I've ever had. But according to Georgia, I'm supposed to have walked away on a high note."

Rick was really beginning to like this Georgia with the big hair and red lips. He and Georgia apparently saw eye-to-eye in the relationship department, and not just for selfish reasons. Given what he'd heard about Jessie's last two years, putting her love life on hold sounded like pretty sage advice. It was the exact same thing he'd decided for himself after his most recent disaster.

"Well, if you're telling me last night needs to be the end of it, I can respect your wishes." Words spoken from his more sensible side, though his other half pouted.

"She thinks I have a problem separating sex and love. That it's gotten me hooked on too many wrong men." Then she turned and raised a half smile. "She thought it might be good for me to try a few one-night stands. To separate the heart from the body so my brain can start making better choices."

He understood the logic. Should actually be reveling in her confession. But he'd gotten stuck on the word *few,* as in *more men than him,* and it left him with a purely illogical stick in his craw. He didn't understand his own possessiveness when it came to her. It was the same reaction he had when he'd woken up this morning alone, that conflicting mix of relief and offense.

He shoved it aside and asked, "Is it working?"

She shook her head. "I don't know. You're my first and this trip I'm taking is breaking the rules. I'm not supposed to be here right now. With you." She glanced at the clock on the dash and he knew what she was thinking even before she asked, "Exactly how late does that pawnshop stay open?"

"It's already closed."

Her lips parted and her expression turned confused. "Then why are we driving to Reno tonight?"

"Because that's where Wade went, and if we're lucky, he's still there."

She snapped her mouth shut, then opened it back up again. "But what if he already pawned my things?"

"Then we'll get them when the shop opens."

They rode in silence for a while as they neared downtown Sacramento. A heavy haze had settled over the skyline, stretching high over the tall buildings like a thin copper cloud. It had been hot today, and Reno would be hotter. Rick wasn't partial to the high desert, particularly not in the dead of summer, and it gave him one more reason to dread this trip.

"If we need to stay the night, we'll get separate rooms," he said.

Her tone took on an edge. "Is that what you want?"

No, it wasn't what he wanted. What he wanted was his life back the way it should have been before her husband decided to play three's company last night. And if he couldn't have that, he wanted Jessie naked all over again, finishing up the business they'd started and maybe making some new business in the process.

But instead, he voiced what he knew he should. "I want what's best for both of us."

How was that for control of Olympic proportions?

"And two rooms is best for both of us."

"You're the one with the rules."

The moment the words slipped out, he wished he could snatch them back. It was a bad answer, one that put control of their situation in her hands. Now all she had to do was say she wanted to break the rules and he'd be stuck having to either play the rejecter or go along and head down the path he knew they shouldn't. The comment had been a slipup, an absentminded response brought on by the fact that she'd crossed her legs and now he couldn't stop trailing his eyes or thoughts into the dark recess between her thighs.

He quickly tried to regroup. "I think Georgia had the right idea."

It had been the correct thing to say. Obviously neither of them needed the complication of another person in their lives. Unfortunately Jessie didn't seem to appreciate the effort, because her mood quickly shifted from apprehension to insult.

"If it was that whole thing about separating sex and love, you don't have to worry. That's Georgia's analysis, not mine." Then she fluttered those long eyelashes and huffed. "I'd hardly go falling head over heels in one weekend."

"That's comforting."

She crossed her arms over her chest, deepening the cleavage pouring out of those doubled-up T-shirts and irritating him even more.

"I was only making conversation," she said tersely. "I mean, you and me…" She let the comment trail off with a laugh.

"What's that supposed to mean?"

She snorted. "Sorry, but you're a little grumpy for my taste."

"Your husband stole my car!"

"*Ex!* And something tells me you're just naturally grumpy no matter what."

His temples began to pulse. "I don't recall being grumpy last night."

"Of course not. There isn't a man who could stay grouchy when a woman's got her mouth all over his—"

He shot up a hand. "Okay! You're right. I'm a miserable sonofabitch."

Jutting her chin toward her passenger-side window, she mumbled, "Now, I never said that."

"But I am. It's true." Then easing the sourness from his tone, he admitted, "I'm not a happy man, Jess."

She turned those caramel eyes back to his. "And why is that? I mean, look at you. You're drop-dead gorgeous. You've got a nice house and a good job. You've got a big-screen TV and a satellite dish on your roof. Isn't that every man's dream? Yet you walk around with a look on your face like you're constantly sniffing cow dung." She turned back to the window and muttered, "Sheesh, you act as though someone died."

The pulse in his temples turned to a throb and he clenched his teeth, not at all interested in continuing this conversation.

So he didn't. Instead he let the comment hang in the air, and it ended up being a tactical mistake Jessie didn't miss.

In a voice filled with too much intuition, she said, "Someone *did* die."

"Change the subject."

She touched a hand to her lips. "Oh. Who was it, a girlfriend?"

"I'm serious."

"Or was it—"

"I said change the subject!"

His sharp snap made her jump, and though he kept his gaze straight on the road ahead, he could feel her eyes burning a hole in him.

He hated talking about Natalie. Hated the pity. The awkward fumbling for the right thing to say, as if some cute

Hallmark phrase could bring the love of his life back. He hated the free advice everyone tried to dole out. Or worse, the ones who claimed to understand how he felt because they'd lost an aunt or a parent or a beloved hamster once. Like their mutual loss gave them a goddamned kinship.

Talking about her always seemed to make her die all over again, and it angered him that Jessie had reached in and pulled out his past so easily. But the farther they drove down the highway, the louder the silence grew, almost screaming at him from the void.

He glanced over at her. She'd gone back to toying with the beads on her necklace, but her face showed nothing that resembled pity or even anger that he'd yelled. Only the simple perusal of the scenery as they began their ascent toward the Sierras.

And in an odd way, her manner calmed him. Or maybe it only made him feel like a cad. Either way, he coughed through the tightness in his throat and explained, "My wife, Natalie, was killed almost three years ago."

She turned to him. "Killed?"

"Sniper on I-80. The guy got his jollies popping off cars one afternoon. Killed two people and wounded another before he took off down the hill."

"Your wife was shot?"

"Rear-ended by an eighteen-wheeler. The twelve-car pile up that resulted from the shootings killed three more. Nat was one of them."

He kept his eyes on the road, not interested in seeing the sad and horrified look that was surely on her face. It was the typical reaction he got when he divulged the details of his wife's death.

"You caught the bastard, right?"

The angry tone had him shifting his gaze to hers. It would have been the first thing he'd asked if the tables had been turned, but funny how few people went straight to that point.

He shook his head. "The case has been cold for over a year."

Only then did she lower her chin and mutter, "I'm sorry. That's got to be hell."

"That about sums it up."

They rode in silence for a while, toward the foothills where the highway met the Sierras and the congested Sacramento suburbs began to give way to rich, dense evergreens. The air was cooling, and he took advantage by lowering his window farther and breathing in the fresh evening air.

"Had you been together long?" she finally asked.

"We were high school sweethearts. We both played basketball. Hung out in the gym a lot."

"I take it you didn't have kids?"

His throat thickened. "We didn't make it that far."

From the corner of his eye he saw sympathy in her gaze as she softly placed a hand to his thigh. "I'm sorry."

And when she pulled it back, he nodded and checked the clock. They still had more than two hours to go, and now that he'd confessed his tragedy, he knew it would seem like five. He'd been through this over and over again, and it was always the same. She'd go weird on him. Hesitant in her fears over what she should or shouldn't say and how she should act.

On the force, he could point to the exact moment a new coworker heard what had happened to him. The casual ease in their eyes would change. The light banter would end. They'd stop griping about their spouses in front of him, keep their conversations to the weather and what they did on the weekends, and in general, treat him as if he was made of fricking eggshells.

He hated it. Had never dreamed how far-reaching his life would be altered, not only by the loss of Natalie but by the constant reminder that he somehow required special handling.

There were only a few people in his life who knew about his past but still treated him like a regular guy. Kevin Fong, Captain Jameson, his best friend from school, Paul Morton. It was a very short list. A number he could count on one hand.

And then Jessica Beane surprised him with a comment that made him wonder if he could add one more.

"Well, I haven't eaten all day. So if I've got to spend my evening dealing with your grouchiness, the least you can do is feed me."

8

IF THERE WAS EVER a candidate for happy pills, Rick Marshall should be first in line for the clinical trials.

Not that Jessie didn't feel for him. No one should have to lose a loved one in such a horrible way, and her heart went out to him for the loss he'd suffered. But that was nearly three years ago. And between the snap to his tone and the frigid shoulder he'd been turning ever since Jess had brought up his wife, she suspected he worked hard to keep those old wounds fresh.

Which was sad. If he and his wife had loved each other as much as he let on, Jessie doubted the woman would have wanted him to die along with her. But she could see by the sturdy shield that darkened his gaze, that's exactly what he'd done.

Peering over the top of her dinner menu, she eyed him across the big oak table, wondering how long he would sit at the restaurant in silence if he wasn't forced to talk. He'd had his nose between the plastic-coated pages since he'd told their server he needed more time. That was almost ten minutes ago. Jessie bet they'd eat the whole meal in silence if left up to him, and a side of her wanted to prove her assumption by keeping her trap shut. Problem was she was never good at the silent treatment. And she certainly wasn't adept at putting up with people who chose to spend their lives feeling sorry for themselves.

Snapping the menu shut, she smiled brightly. "Well, I know what I'm having." When he didn't respond, she added, "I'm going for the jumbo bacon cheeseburger, medium rare, with fries, a large Coke and a side of onion rings."

That managed to conjure up a grunt.

"I almost went for the chili cheese dog," she said, "but I'm spoiled by the ones they sell at the Colbrook County Fair. I've yet to find a dog that comes anywhere close to those, especially here in California."

Getting the distinct impression she was talking to herself, she pushed on. "I hate to be one of those out-of-towners who says everything's better back home, but it is true about everything being bigger in Texas. Not only are the dogs bigger but it's *not* a chili cheese dog if it's *not* made with real Texas chili."

"Mmm-hmm," he muttered from behind the menu before he slapped it shut and set it on top of hers.

She met his gaze, trying to ignore the little sizzle those eyes sent up the back of her spine. They were even more lethal when combined with his half-cocked smile, but she doubted she'd be seeing that anytime soon. She supposed that was a good thing. No sense in getting hot flashes over a man who'd already made it clear they wouldn't repeat last night's marathon.

Though in her opinion that decision was still on the table.

He'd been too quick to jump on the idea of their getting separate rooms. And no way would she buy the notion that he hadn't enjoyed himself as much as she had, no matter how badly the morning after had fouled things up. Besides, the more time Jessie spent with him, the more she suspected that what Rick said and what Rick wanted were two entirely different things. And if she couldn't get him to lighten up with conversation, she'd resort to the tactic she'd already proven successful.

Because one thing was for sure. No way would she spend the rest of her weekend in Reno with Mr. Grumpity-Grump and this foul mood.

"So what are you having, besides sour grapes?" she asked.

Oddly the crack seemed to brighten his stony face. "I have the right to be angry. If you recall, I shouldn't even have to be doing this."

"That was this morning and I've already apologized. Twice." She grabbed her napkin and placed it in her lap. "What have I done to you lately?"

His brow flicked an answer she couldn't read, but before he could follow it up with words, they were interrupted by their server.

"Are you two ready to order?"

"Sure," he said. "I'll have the club sandwich with a side salad, blue cheese dressing and a glass of ice water. The lady will have a jumbo bacon cheeseburger, medium rare, with fries, a large Coke and a side of onion rings."

He glanced at Jess without an ounce of smugness even though he knew she hadn't thought he'd been paying attention.

She'd forgotten she was sitting with a cop.

"Anything else?" the woman asked.

They both shook their heads and the tall brunette tucked her pen in her apron, promising to bring their drinks before sauntering off.

Meeting his gaze across the table, it wasn't difficult for Jessie to imagine them together under different circumstances. One that involved him happy and her on a date. It would be nice to be involved with a decent guy for a change. And despite the hostile and critical front he put up, Jessie knew that deep down, Rick had to be one of the good ones. She'd seen him with that couple at the station, how he'd stayed calm and reassuring even though the woman's sobs put panic in his eyes.

Rick cared about people. Maybe too much.

"What have you done to me lately?" he repeated. "The statute of limitations hasn't expired on my stolen car."

"That was hours ago, and I'm positive I've done nothing to upset your life since then." When he opened his mouth to object, she quickly added, "And don't go there. You and I both know you would have been miserable driving all this way without me."

"I would have been in Reno by now."

"If you're referring to this meal stop, you have to eat, and downing fast-food burgers while driving is dangerous. Face it, I'm helping you out."

He pulled his cell phone, used to replace the one he'd had stolen, out of his jacket and flicked it open. "Not yet, but you will." He scooted to the edge of the booth then stood. "I need to call my partner. While I'm gone you need to come up with a list of all the people back home who might know where your husband is."

"Ex!"

"It's time to start making some calls."

She watched him stroll down the aisle and out the front door, little mini cyclones twisting through her belly as she eyed that firm butt with the memory of how she'd dug her fingers into it last night about this time.

Oh, what a difference a day made. Twenty-four hours

ago she'd been on top of the world, enjoying the physical pleasure of a hot, rugged cop whose only purpose in life was to bring her to orgasm then leave her shuddering and begging for more. They'd fit together like butter on bread, her moves bringing relief to his haunted, tortured eyes, and his gentle caresses nurturing a soul that longed to be cherished and touched.

They'd been good together. Good for each other. And though Rick would like to erase the evening from the history books, Jessie concluded that what they really needed was a repeat instead.

Pulling the cell phone from her purse, she dialed Georgia and waited, crossing her fingers that her best friend would be there before Rick came back.

"Hello?"

She breathed a sigh of relief. "Georgia, I'm so glad I caught you."

"Jess? Are you all right?"

"Yes, I'm fine. But I need a big favor."

"What's up? Where are you?"

She paused while the server set a large icy glass of soda in front of her and water with a sprig of lemon for Rick. And when the woman walked away, she lowered her voice, keeping one eye peeled on the front door.

"I'm in Truckee. We stopped for dinner and I don't have much time. I need you to do something for me."

"Sure, what is it?"

"I need you to call some hotels in Reno and get me a room. We'll be spending the night tonight."

"*A* room?" Georgia asked, with the emphasis on the singular. "Where's Rick sleeping?"

She smiled. "If I have my way, he won't be sleeping at all."

"Bad idea, Jess. That was supposed to be a one-night stand."

Jessie suspected Georgia would react this way, and for a brief moment, she considered lying and saying Rick could find his own room. But she was a grown woman. Too old to be sneaking around behind anyone's back, particularly her best friend.

"So it will be a two-night stand. Hardly any difference at all."

"It's a huge difference. I already don't like you spending the weekend with this guy. You're going to get attached like you always do. It wasn't supposed to turn out this way."

"Tell me about it. But trust me, the sheriff is light years from relationship material. I won't be coming home starry-eyed and in love. In fact, my plan is a desperate attempt to tolerate his existence until we can get home and part ways."

"Your plan? What do you mean, plan?"

"I'll tell you the whole story when I get home tomorrow. In the meantime, would you please call around and find us a room? There's some big event going on in town and I'm thinking most of the casinos might be booked." In fact, she was banking on it. Grabbing her Coke, she took a quick sip then explained, "I'm on the road without a phone book and the roaming charges alone are going to kill me. Any hotel will do."

Georgia sighed. "I don't like this. Your track record—"

"Was left behind when I moved to California. I'm a big girl now with a much wiser head on my shoulders."

After a long pause, she heard Georgia huff. "I'll find a place and call you back."

Jessie grinned. "You're my best friend in the whole world."

"Yeah, yeah."

"We're in the mountains so if you can't get through leave the info on my voice mail." And when she spied Rick coming back through the door, she quickly said goodbye and hung up the phone.

He slid into the booth then eyed her phone as she tucked it back in her purse. "Tell me you've got good news."

Oh, she had good news all right. Her strong and studly dinner companion was about to get multiple orgasms before the night was through. And with a normal hot-blooded man, she'd share that newsflash with him right now, allowing them to spend their meal making a to-do list of sexual fantasies they'd fulfill once they got alone. Unfortunately Rick Marshall was far from normal.

If she didn't figure out a way to lighten him up she'd go stir-crazy before noon tomorrow. It was time she put that zing back in his eyes and the sexy smile on his lips.

But he didn't need to know that just yet.

"I'd only been checking my messages," she said.

"And I take it you didn't get any more calls from Wade."

She shook her head and his mood darkened—if that were actually possible.

The server came with their meals and Jessie quickly dug in, starved from not eating a morsel of anything since last night's dinner.

"According to my partner, Wade hasn't used my cell phone again," Rick muttered. "Battery's probably dead."

"And the cops haven't found your car yet, I take it."

His frown said no. He slathered a dollop of mayonnaise on his sandwich before placing the bread back on top and taking a big bite. "Who can you call?" he asked through a mouthful of food.

Though the last thing Jessie wanted to do was chat with any of Wade's old friends, she supposed she owed it to Rick to do whatever she could to help track Wade down.

She shrugged and pulled a loose piece of bacon from her burger. "I'd have to give it some thought."

Rick looked at her as if she were crazed. "Exactly how long were you two married?"

"Three years, if you count the year we spent dealing with the cops and the creditors and getting a divorce. I suppose that would make two good ones."

He washed his food down with water and sat back. "So? What about his parents, or your parents? Best friends? Who did he hang out with?"

Taking a stroll down memory lane wasn't Jessie's idea of a good time, especially since she'd spent the last year trying to forget every one of those days.

Rick hadn't been the only one in the world to lose his future. When Wade's life came crashing down, her dreams had shattered with it. Gone was the loving, hardworking man she thought she'd married and in his place was a sour, shameless criminal.

The moment charges had been brought against him, Jessie had cooperated with the authorities, telling them everything she knew and giving them any evidence they'd requested. Wade had considered it a breach of their marriage and had turned on her like a light, becoming cruel and angry, as if she were the cause of all his troubles—not to mention conveniently ignoring the fact that he'd lied to her since the day they met.

Wade was supposed to have been her savior. The man who took her from the turbulence that was her life at home and gave her the opportunity to make a real home of her own. They'd bought a house with a yard and a dog. She'd gotten a secretarial job at a medical billing firm with decent pay and good benefits. Benefits she'd need when she and her upstanding business owner of a husband decided to have children of their own.

For the first time in her life, she'd found normalcy and the hope that she could build the kind of caring haven that she'd lost when her father died.

Until she discovered it had all been built on a lie, and her loving husband and happy home had been nothing more than a ticking time bomb waiting to explode.

She eyed Rick, who sat there patiently waiting for her to answer, and she literally fumbled trying to consider who Wade might still be close to. Unlike Rick, she didn't care to hang on to the devastating moments in her past, and she'd worked hard ever since to stop dwelling on her misfortune and build a new life for herself.

Mentally stepping back through those days wasn't as quick as he presumed it should be.

"Well," she said. "His two closest friends went to jail with him. I have no idea where they are or if they've been released."

He pulled a small pad and pen from his pocket and began jotting notes, the scene reminiscent of the questioning she'd had to endure after Wade's arrest.

"Give me names."

She did, and then went on. "His parents won't speak to me. They're of the opinion I was a family traitor for telling the police everything I knew."

He looked up, and in his eyes she saw that sympathy he'd shown the old couple at the station. Was this his practiced cop look, or did he really care about what she'd gone through?

"They sound real swell," he said.

Her throat began to close. It was exactly why she liked to keep the past where it belonged…in the past.

"They blamed me for all of it. Said Wade's whole life of crime was only to provide me with the kind of home I'd wanted. Now they won't forgive me for what happened to their poor child."

This from the people who'd welcomed her into their family and treated her like the daughter they never had.

"What about your parents?" he asked. "Does he talk to any of your friends or relatives?"

Jessie snorted. "My mother's no better. She was raised by the Tammy Wynette song, 'Stand By Your Man.' She believes in for better or worse no matter what."

Now Rick's expression turned to shock. "Don't tell me she expected you to stay married."

She nodded. "I'm a grave disappointment."

"You're kidding me."

"Oh, no. My mother's very loyal when it comes to the institution of marriage." Which was why her childhood had been just a notch above hell.

Granted, her stepfather never physically abused her or her mother, but he was hardly a provider and their marriage had been far from loving. Jessie's mother worked her fingers to the bone to supplement the pension they received from the army after her father died, and Ray Beane found all kinds of ways to spend it. Instead of earning an honest wage, the man fell into every get-rich-quick scheme he came across on late-night TV and in the back pages of magazines. Nine out of ten of them were scams that cost the family their savings. The one or two that did pan out got frittered away on the next one.

There'd been no stability in her life. One day they were driving a shiny new Cadillac and the next the repo man was hauling it away and they were moving back to the double-wide her grandmother owned as a rental. It had become the circle of her existence, the lessons learned being that she could only count on herself and that the only way to keep hope for the future was to never, ever look back.

"Look," she said. "Rather than ruin my meal by opening that can of worms, why don't I promise that between here and Reno, I'll try to get in touch with a couple of people back home, see if anyone's heard from Wade. And in the meantime, I'll eat in peace."

His eyes held nothing but sincerity and understanding as he nodded and dug into his salad.

Jessie looked down at her food, now only marginally interested in the meal, but she forced herself to eat. Later, when they got to Reno and found their hotel, she'd need her strength. Because she knew for a fact that once she started making calls back home, Rick wouldn't be the only one in need of some sexual release. With her granna Hawley gone, there wasn't much left for Jessie in Texas, and what was there wasn't pleasant.

She picked up a slice of pickle and eyed him while she popped it in her mouth, letting the tangy taste wash the gloom from her spirit. Nothing would go further in easing her anxiety than running her hands along his silky, naked back. To taste his flesh, inhale that rough, salty scent and feel him harden and grow inside her. To anticipate the explosion, gorge in the urgent feast and bask in the ultimate rapture. And then to do it again and again until all the demons had been exorcised and they could lie together in the glory of two beings cleansed and fed.

9

RICK DIDN'T KNOW what he'd expected. He knew better than to believe he'd get lucky and find Wade and his Charger parked by the side of the road the moment they pulled off the freeway into Reno. He figured he wouldn't stumble upon the man at the Quick Mart, or pull in behind him at the Starbucks drive-through. He knew Reno was a big town with lots of people and lots of cars.

But he hadn't expected this.

This was a madhouse. Insanity personified within the square miles of the city's main drag.

Kevin had said something about a quarter million people coming in from all over the country for Hot August Nights. What had Rick thought a quarter million people would look like, prom night at the local high school?

If anyone questioned America's love affair with the automobile, this was the place to confirm it. He'd never seen so many hot rod cars and trucks and buggies, poodle skirts and ponytails, chrome wheels and pompadours, Elvises and Marilyns.

And it was after 10:00 p.m.

What would this place look like during the day when the rest of the town was awake and celebrating?

"Is that it up there?" Jessie asked, walking three paces

ahead of him. With a cruise going on down Virginia Street, they'd had to abandon the vehicle and head out on foot to get anywhere near the pawnshop Wade had called. And even walking, they found themselves snaking through the eclectic crowd on the sidewalk mulling around to watch the hot rods go by.

A celebration of the fifties and sixties, Hot August Nights appeared to bring an odd array of people into town, from old-timers who were reliving their teens, to all their generations after. Most seemed to come for the costumes and the cars, though a section of the younger crowd looked to be here for the party. The heat had stripped the younger women of most of their clothes, combining with the gambling and alcohol, a subculture of sex and seduction that played in tune to the music of the rumbling engines and squealing wheels.

No wonder the cops were busy.

But even in this smorgasbord of ages, shapes and sizes, the prettiest woman on the street was still Jessica Beane.

He followed her up the sidewalk as she gracefully snaked through the crowd, those silky red curls bouncing at her shoulders and parting at her neck when caught by the occasional warm breeze.

He loved that she didn't try to tame them with straightening tools or gel. Anything controlled simply wouldn't be Jessie. Just like the clothing she wore revealed the woman underneath. Simple, but sexy. Plain with an added touch of flamboyance. She kept her soul on her sleeve, said what she meant and did what she wanted. And in a span of twenty-four hours, Rick couldn't temper his respect and admiration for her no matter how hard he tried.

Lengthening his stride when she disappeared behind a

crowd, he found her standing at the window of the pawn-shop, cupping her eyes to the glass.

He glanced down at the decal on the door. "They're closed until Monday."

She took two paces to the right and surveyed what she could of the dark room, as though she expected to see her friend's ring sitting in a display case at the counter. "I can't believe they'd stay closed through the weekend during this Hot Rod Nights thing." Then she dropped her hands and turned to him, those sweet eyes dimmed with disappointment. "Look at this place." She waved a hand over the crowd. "There's got to be thousands of people losing their shirts in the casinos right now. How could a pawnshop be closed on a weekend?"

Rick shook his head in agreement.

"I can't leave until this place opens and I find out if Georgia's ring is in there," she said.

He couldn't, either. Since finding Wade in this town had gone from a long shot to a last chance, Rick's only hope was that Wade had found the laptop in the trunk and pawned it, too. And in case he hadn't, the woman at his side had now become his only connection to finding the man anytime soon.

He looked up and down the busy street, praying through some impossibility he'd see Wade casually strolling by. "When do you think we might hear from some of the people you called?" he asked.

Her disappointment deepened. "Possibly never. Back when he was arrested, the whole town acted as though I single-handedly brought Wade down, including my own family. I called the couple of people who had sided with me at the time, but it's been a year. Their attitudes could have been poisoned by now."

She shifted and leaned against the glass, running her fingers through those curls to shove a few wayward strands from her face. Rick's hands ached to do that for her. In fact, his hands ached to do a lot of things, including wiping that heavy weight off her shoulders and morphing her back into the sexy, excited woman he'd been with last night.

The mere fleeting thought of the encounter stiffened his cock. All day, he'd been trying to hold on to every reason he had to be angry with her, to blame her for his troubles, to rue the night they'd shared. And instead, all she'd done was endear herself to him and make his body yearn for more.

As much as he wished it weren't so, he didn't rue their night. He thanked the heavens for it. And like a flu that starts off with a cough in the morning and has you bull-dozed by night, his lust for Jessie had only compounded, despite all his efforts to thwart it.

And now it looked as if he wouldn't be away from her anytime soon. How was he supposed to survive that?

He started by shoving his hands in his pockets. They'd fit themselves too easily over those two supple breasts and needed to be contained before he lost all control.

"We're going to have to find a place to stay," he reluctantly admitted. Then glancing up and down the main drag, he shook his head. "I don't know if that's going to be possible."

A smile curved her lips and sunk a dimple into one cheek. "Now, this is the part where you thank me." Pushing away from the building, she stepped toward him and motioned them both back toward the block where he'd parked his rental car. "Back in Truckee, I put Georgia to the task of finding us rooms for the night."

His mood brightened. "You got us rooms?"

"One," she said as she swept past him, leaving that spicy

scent in his nostrils and that tight, round bottom in his view. "The Starbright Casino out by the airport. I've got the address on my voice mail. It was the only place with a cancellation and we've snagged it."

"One room," he said, shoving his hands deeper in his pockets. Any further and he'd be dragging his knuckles at his knees like the Neanderthal he felt like right then.

She tossed a casual glance over her shoulder. "I know we'd discussed two, but as you can see, the town's a little busy this weekend. The good news is Georgia said it's got two double beds." She stopped and turned. "So if you're worried about our earlier agreement, we'll only be sharing a bathroom." Then she trailed a slim finger around a button at his chest, the simple touch rushing waves of heat through his veins. "I can be good. Can you?"

No. No, he couldn't. In fact, everything about Jessica Beane made him want to be bad. Hell, he still had the taste of those moist lips on his tongue and the feel of those silky legs on his fingertips. He still had a half-dozen ideas in his head of things they hadn't gotten to, not to mention that slice of unfinished business from when he'd woken up alone.

Ever since his last climax he'd been building steam for another round, their time together today only compressing and condensing it into a force on the verge of explosion.

Could he be good?

Oh, he and Jessica Beane could be very, very good.

But it didn't change reality. Aside from lust and some friendly affection, he was an emotional wasteland, no good for any woman and most certainly no good for Jessie. She had a mountain of problems and he couldn't solve a solitary one. Adding one more was nothing short of cruel, particularly given what her friend Georgia had said about her mixing love and sex.

Normally Rick wouldn't consider her emotions his business. She was an adult and he'd been honest. That was all he owed her. But despite her gritty temper and stiff, worthy spine, there was a vulnerability in her eyes he couldn't ignore. Life had hurt her one too many times, and he didn't want to be the latest in a string of disappointments.

He'd already put enough of those upon himself.

He swallowed and her brow coiled in concern. Or was it mischief? "Really, Sheriff. No one does anything they don't want to do," she said.

Easier said than done, he thought, before he pulled a hand from his pocket and placed it at the base of her back. "Let's go," he said.

The walk to the car was thick with tension, the drive out to the casino torture. Two beds in one room. That wasn't enough distance. In fact, with the scent of her sex still lingering in his thoughts, he doubted separate hotels would be enough to keep them apart. But he tried to focus on the big picture and remind himself that he was a civilized man, a trained cop. And Jessie was just a woman, not a power he couldn't conquer.

He focused on Creed Thornton and the image of that smug grin stamped on his face. Rick opted for the worst in order to work up the anger to stay focused. Thorton hadn't a care in the world now that he'd snuffed out his sex toy and their illegitimate child. He'd no doubt gone on to new servants, this time probably being more careful with condoms if only for the savings in legal fees.

He ripped Jessie from his thoughts and replaced her

with the sight of the Mendozas, pained and fearful that their precious gift was taken with no one to pay the price.

Then he remembered that this trip was about fixing a bad situation instead of creating a new one. And by the time they reached the front desk, he felt calmed, if only slightly.

"You have a reservation for Jessica Beane?" Jessie said as they reached the check-in clerk.

The air was smoky and all around them was the sound of slot machine bells, heavy coins dropping in metal, the *tick-tick-tick* of gambling wheels and distant cheers of happy winners. Waitresses were half-dressed, bringing free drinks for anyone dumping their cash on the tables or in the machines, and aside from the large, glass doors at the entrance, there wasn't another window to be found.

Nor were there any clocks.

This was a place where time stopped and the world outside ceased to exist. It was a festival of light and sound, of hope and fantasy, with dreams of riches and tastes of the forbidden.

And standing so close to Jessie, those shapely bare legs extending out of that green-apple skirt and down to calf-shaping heels, his lesser side wanted to be swept into it all and go along for the ride.

So he kept the Mendozas at the front of his thoughts, imagining him having to tell them that he had nothing. That the case had gone cold, which certainly meant their daughter's death would go unpunished. He held on to that feeling of failure and frustration, aware that avoiding that scenario was more important than sex and drinks and fantasies.

It gave him the strength to ask, "Do you have any additional rooms available?"

The reservations clerk eyed them both curiously then

shook her head. "I'm sorry. We've been booked solid for months. It's a miracle you got the room you have. Even cancellations are going within minutes. You just happened to pick the perfect time to check back when you did earlier today."

Jessie couldn't hide the irritation in her eyes when she took the key card and slid her bank card across the counter, but Rick didn't care. This trip was about business and needed to stay that way.

Quickly he snatched her card from the counter and replaced it with his own.

"You don't have to—" Jessie started.

"I'm not. It's on the SFPD."

With Reno only a few hours from San Francisco, they hadn't thought to pack for an overnight stay. So they stopped in the hotel gift shop for toiletries before making their way to the room.

"Is the idea of sharing a room with me really that repulsive?" she asked when they stepped into the elevator. She pressed the button for their floor and moved to the side.

"Hardly."

The mirrored walls gave him a 360-degree view he didn't need. Eyeing the right corner, he could get a glimpse of cleavage, breasts and ass all in one scoop. The dim light darkened her features and put a sparkle in those honey eyes, and Rick concluded this also was a casino feature designed to set the mood. This one for sex, as couples checked their reflections, gathered up a few ideas and headed for their rooms.

He swallowed a lump in his throat and darted his eyes to the floor.

"I already told you. No one does anything they don't want to do," she said.

He shot her a glance. "Interesting how you keep phrasing it that way."

As if she knew what this small space was doing to him, she placed her hands on her breasts and adjusted her blouse, pumping up the cleavage while licking her lips in the mirror. She'd made the move with pure innocence in her eyes. Nothing more than a woman who couldn't resist making some corrections to her clothing when tempted with floor-to-ceiling mirrors.

Except there was nothing innocent about that move. She knew exactly what she was doing, and it was working like a charm.

When she wiggled her ass and straightened her skirt, his cock turned to concrete.

"Phrase what?" she asked.

"That we don't do anything we don't want to do." He cleared the frog in his throat with a sharp cough. "As if the matter wasn't already closed."

"Was it?" she tossed over her shoulder as the doors opened to their floor and she stepped into the hall.

He stiffly followed. "Why do I get the feeling I'm being played?"

As casual as a fox, she rounded the corner, then another before she answered his accusation. "Chief, it's simple. This entire town is booked. I found a room. We both need to sleep and shower."

When she came to the door, she slid the key in the slot and pushed it open.

A musty smell greeted them, but Rick barely noticed. When she flicked on the light, his eyes and thoughts went straight to the two double beds lined against the wall, separated only by a foot of space and a side table.

It wasn't enough. He needed a cement barrier. Maybe some barbed wire and a couple armed guards at the corners of the room. And even then, it would only leave him with a fighting chance.

"We both need a lot of things," he muttered under his breath, and Jessie's smile said she'd heard him loud and clear.

Tossing her purse on the table, she kicked off her heels and groaned in ecstasy as she dug her toes into the carpet. Then she unclipped her belt and wiggled out of the skirt she'd just adjusted in the elevator.

Now the only thing separating his hands from her sex was a thin black thong.

His mouth went dry.

"What are you doing?" he asked in a voice that sounded as if he'd just smoked a pack of Camels.

"Getting comfortable." She stretched her arms above her and exposed that luscious belly button he'd circled his tongue around less than twenty-four hours ago. "That was a long drive. It's been a long day. My legs are cramped, my feet are killing me, and ever since that meal we had back in Truckee, my skirt has felt two sizes too small."

Bending over to touch her toes, she spoke between her knees. "I'm unwinding."

"No, you're not. You're torturing me."

He could have sworn he saw a gratified smirk on those lips before he yanked his eyes away from that silky, bare ass and headed for the minibar. Then he remembered he didn't drink anymore and his mood soured. Instead he stepped to the window—the only place in the room where he could keep his back to her without making it look obvious. He opened the curtains to a view of the parking lot below and tried to focus on the cars instead of the half-naked sexpot behind him.

Then he heard the toss of more clothing.

"Now, there's an idea I can run with."

"What idea?" he asked, his cock growing harder at the mere thought of her topless.

"Torture."

Another toss of something then a snap and Rick had heard about enough. It was time to take control of the situation. But when he turned to face her and found her standing there unabashedly naked, her slim hands on those curvy hips and those breasts perked and ready for his palms, the control he'd mustered slid through his veins in a snapping trail of sparks.

Damn, she was beautiful.

Double-damn, she was the sexiest thing he'd ever seen. And with every second of their evening together replaying through his mind like a forbidden sex video, he doubted he would get through this night without sinking into her body one more time. Or maybe three.

Stepping over to the bag of toiletries she'd bought, she reached in, pulled out a handful of foil packets and tossed them on the bed.

When had she chosen those?

"You see, Sheriff, what you've been doing is torturing me with that rotten mood. Now it looks like I'm going to have to put up with it for at least one or two more days."

Leaving the condoms on the bed like a little pile of promises, she casually crossed the room, stepped to the bathroom and flicked on the light.

"Personally," she went on, "the only time I happen to like you is when I've got my legs wrapped around your waist. So if I've got to deal with Grouchy Frown Man all day, the least you can do is pleasure me at night."

She moved out of view and he heard the sound of water rushing from the shower before she stepped back to the doorway.

"Like I said, Chief, no one does anything they don't want to do. But I think if we're going to get along for the next forty-eight hours, it might be a good idea if you got naked and joined me in the shower."

Then she disappeared into the bathroom, leaving him standing there with two choices. One involved sleeping in his car and spending the next couple of days with the image of those unused condoms burning a hole in his brain. The other risked taking a bad situation and trashing it further.

"And stop your worrying, Sergeant," she called from the shower. "When we get back to San Francisco, I'll be able to say my goodbyes just fine."

She might. But as he stood there hot and hard, the image of that petite, curvy body slick with suds and slippery sex, he wondered if walking away would be as easy as she thought.

10

JESSIE WOULD officially give Rick sixty more seconds to join her in the shower before she cranked the faucet to cold and doused herself with one big, icy reality check. She'd never been vain enough to think herself irresistible. Though when it came to this man, she could have sworn a little enticement would have brought him back for an encore of the incredible night they'd shared.

Had she totally misread the dark, hungry look in his eyes? Was that bulge behind his fly a figment of her imagination? Wishful thinking by a desperate mind?

She turned her back to the spray and let the warm water massage the tension from her neck. She'd had a dozen better ideas for relaxing away the bad day, but she'd been waiting almost ten minutes now and it was looking like none of them would pan out.

Oh, she could really pick the winners, couldn't she?

Problem was, in her heart, she'd really thought Rick was one of them. It just went to show that Georgia had probably been right. Jessie still had a lot to learn about sex and relationships and which men were right and which were oh, so wrong. It was way more than she could learn from a measly one-night stand, no matter how great.

Turning around, she ducked her head under the water,

grabbed the knob and began to slowly crank down the heat, deciding she'd only stop when she'd sufficiently chilled the ignorance out of her system. That or slipped into a coma from hypothermia. But as the temperature began dipping from warm to tepid, she heard a rustling behind her then two big hands circled her waist.

A quick thrill tickled her spine. "I'd almost given up on you," she said, unable to wipe the smile from her face. So, tonight wasn't going to be as dismal as she'd feared.

She leaned into him, enjoying the sharp contrast between the cool water running over her chest and the hot body at her back. It covered her with gooseflesh and shivers that had more to do with the man than the water.

"Impatient, aren't you?"

His warm breath licked against her ear and brought a wobble to her knees.

"Would you have me any other way?"

He kissed a path to her nape. "I'll have you a number of ways before the night is through."

He drew her against his waist, his stiff erection backing up his words, and her sex swelled with anticipation. She'd wanted her red-hot lover again, and it seemed he'd arrived with bells on. And as a slow burn boiled in her belly, she knew this night would be every bit as pleasurable as the last.

Gently he began working her with his lips and hands, caressing her taut nipples, dipping down between her thighs and back again. He leveled his legs against hers and held her close, playing her body like a fine cello. His fingers strummed chords through her veins that crept up her throat in deep moans and sharp gasps.

"I like this," he whispered, and she smiled at the lusty desire in his voice.

She liked it, too. Liked it much more than spending the day in a car with Mr. Angry At The World, his low groans and smooth touches expressing the side of Rick Marshall Jessie wished would stick around. Granted, today hadn't been the best day for either of them. But something told her this sexy, playful side of Rick didn't come out as often as it should. She hoped maybe this time she could make his good mood last.

Cool water sluiced between them, trickling down her back in rivers of chilly sensation. She lolled her head against his shoulder, letting her thoughts drift away from this roller-coaster day and all the trouble that lay ahead.

Taking a tiny bar of soap in his palm, he tilted the shower head and began smoothing suds all over her, rubbing a slick lather over her breasts and down her back, around her thighs toward the sweet spot that had begun aching for attention. He lifted her hand and licked the pulse at her wrist, trailing his tongue in small circles, before moving to the next spot, leaving a path of tingles in its wake.

His moves were agonizingly slow, his hard cock slicking up and down her back, weakening her limbs while his hands and mouth teased every sensitive spot on her flesh. Her blood heated. Her sex throbbed. She wanted more of the cool water, but he'd positioned the spray to deliver only a fine mist. Not enough to temper the surge through her pulse or the hot fire building between her legs.

Lower he went, massaging her thighs, then her calves, stopping to take a bite of her ass before digging his fingers in and kneading the soft flesh. Inch by tortuous inch he moved closer to her sex. She braced her hands against the shower wall and parted her thighs in invitation, her heart rate mounting as he moved in and under then finally to the place she needed him most.

"Yessss," she hissed when those sudsy fingers reached her sensitized nub, and he responded with a chuckle laced with evil and sin.

"Is this what you want, sexy?" he asked, slipping a finger up inside so there was no mistaking his intent.

She arched her back to give him access and he slid a second finger inside before smoothing his thumb between her folds, circling her clit while he used his other hand to tease her taut nipples.

Liquid heat ran through her. "Oh, yes."

He pressed those warm lips to her ear. "Do you want to come, baby?"

He increased the speed, moving closer to her nub. He pulled her up against his chest, his strong breath and heavy heartbeat thudding loudly, letting her know she wasn't the only one getting off right now. Allowing her body to fall against him, she wiggled her back against his cock and smiled when he moaned and joined in the rhythm.

"Yeah," she urged. "I want us both to come."

Grasping her tightly, he stroked repeatedly, sinking his teeth into her shoulder then kissing the spot, finding another place to bite then kissing it again. It went on and on, stroking, kissing, licking and tormenting until her body swelled and ached, mere inches from climax.

She scraped her nails against the tile as the waves of pleasure grew, increasing in depth, sucking the breath from her lungs and the strength from her limbs. She was close. Oh, so close. And her low groan of warning told him she had almost reached the edge.

Their bodies rubbed and grooved, two slippery, sudsy forms grinding together from ankles to wrists, almost dancing in the cool mist of the dim shower stall.

The Harlequin Reader Service — Here's how it works:

And just as the final swell began to build, he slipped his fingers away and lightly toyed with her breast instead.

"Don't stop," she demanded.

He made a *tsk-tsk* sound, then remarked with a smile in his voice, "So impatient."

She rubbed against him in a desperate move to keep going, but he was having none of it and her body sobbed. Her once heavy eyelids flew open. With her sex pulsing and screaming for release, she curled her toes and shot out a curse. "I was right there."

He kissed the space between her shoulder blades. "And I'll have you there again before we're done."

She tried to turn in his arms, intent on clasping that hard shaft and taking what he denied, but he held her tight, bracing his chest against her spine.

"No cheating," he teased. "Besides, I have a better idea."

He slipped his cock between her cheeks and she gasped as the soapy shaft slid easily between the folds, the soft head stopping short of the entrance to her womb.

"Didn't you accuse me of torturing you before?" he said.

He slid his erection back and forth, teasing around her core without ever slipping in.

"You're torturing me now."

"Just like you've been torturing me all day," he said, his voice filled with pleasure. He stroked the long shaft between her legs, tormenting her with slick sensation before gliding ruefully away. "My cock has been stiff with unfinished business since I woke up to an empty bed this morning."

"Then let's finish it now," she urged.

Smoothing his palm over her mound, he pressed lightly, giving her just enough friction to stay painfully aroused without boiling over. "Oh, we're going to finish it all right. But not until I even the score."

His wicked chuckle pumped heat through her veins, setting her on fire in a mixture of rage, excitement and intrigue. She'd learned last night that her sexy sheriff could be full of surprises, and though a side of her begged her to end this, the adventurer in her wanted to know where this was going.

"I wonder how long I can keep you right there," he whispered, nibbling her ear then thrusting his cock again between her thighs.

"You'll never last," she shot back before realizing the slam would only egg him on, extending her agony further.

Oh, she was in trouble. Delightful, glorious trouble. And he proved it by coiling his arms around her waist and pulling her up to her toes.

Now he slid easily between her folds, brushing his cock against her clit, grazing her swollen nub and sending her to the warning track all over again. He thrust once, twice and again before setting her down and pulling away.

"I've lasted all day, sweetheart. A little more time isn't going to kill me." Then angling the shower spray between them, he added, "But it might kill you."

She broke free and twisted in his arms, the cool water rushing between them, rinsing the suds from their bodies and bringing welcome relief to the stifling heat pooled between her legs. But before she could take advantage, he cupped her face with his big hands and drove his tongue deep into her mouth.

She sucked in a hard breath, feasting greedily as his strong arms wrapped around her and held her close.

She so loved the feel of his embrace, those arms enveloping her with strength. It was the ultimate sense of protection and safety she'd rarely had growing up and had spent her adult life searching for in vain. She'd learned to take these moments and relish them, inhaling his breath and soaking in the comfort of his body wrapped around hers.

If she could stay this way forever, it still wouldn't be long enough.

Breaking the kiss, he pressed his lips in a trail down her neck, lower and lower until he'd reached her breast and took her nipple into his mouth. He slipped a hand between her thighs, circling her slick clit, rushing the sensation back through her veins until she couldn't take it anymore and cried uncle.

"You are," she gasped. "You are going to kill me." He moved his lips to hers, and the dark, burning need in those blue eyes matched the feeling in her chest. "Please," she begged. "I need you in me."

"Are you telling me you've had enough?"

He cupped her mound and squeezed.

"Yes."

"You empathize with my plight?"

"My heart bleeds for the sorry situation I left you in this morning."

His laugh was low and sincere.

"You were mean," he said. "Something about only liking me when your legs are wrapped around my waist."

He bent down and slid his tongue over a nipple. Then he licked and sucked before adding, "Do you know how badly you turn me on? How horny I've been, having to sit in that car next to these long, sexy legs?"

He snaked his hands down her thighs.

"I'm sorry. I'll wear a kimono tomorrow. Please, just put it—"

But the words stuck in her throat when he dipped down and stroked his tongue between her folds.

She backed against the tile wall and wailed, digging her hands through that thick, dark hair and pulling him close.

"Oh, please don't stop."

And with that, he rose and lifted her to him before driving hard inside her.

She cried with pleasure, never in her life being held so sufferingly close to the edge without being granted relief. And now that she had him inside, she wrapped her legs tightly around him, not daring to let him go.

He grunted. Her body sighed. And when he ebbed and thrust again, she curved her back and took him deeper.

"How do you like me now?" he muttered, his face buried against the crook of her neck.

"Oh, I like you a lot."

And it was true. Where Grouchy Cop Rick could be annoying and rude, the man underneath was the best sex she could remember. His thick shaft filled her, bringing glorious sensation to her tortured and aching body. Rivers of cool water sluiced down their chests and nearly evaporated from the heat that burned between them. He drove her long and deep, just the way she wanted it, thrusting and surging, until she nearly sobbed with need. Pleasure crested and ebbed, then crested again, each time going deeper, climbing higher until the final wave spilled up through her throat and erupted in a long, desperate cry.

The end came hard and lasted. Her orgasm sped through her muscles and clenched tightly around his cock until he slammed a fist to the tile and burst with a cry of his own.

For an infinite moment, they gave themselves up to the climax, arms grabbing, legs trembling, hips thrusting until with ragged breath they both slid to the base of the tub.

Jessie reached out and shut off the water then lowered onto his chest, their hearts beating furiously, as they calmed in the shell of the bathtub. Jessie rested her head on his chest and his arms circled around her.

Mist swirled around them as tiny droplets fell from their skin, both of them slick and soaked to the bone. While the shower head ticked off an ever slowing *drip-drip-drip,* she let the air and the heat from her body dry the wetness from her skin. It took a long time before either of them spoke. Jessie was spent and sated, her muscles weak and wobbly from restraint held too long.

"I have to admit," Rick finally said, "this is the first time I've ever had sex that landed me on my back in a bathtub."

"You haven't lived," she mocked, bringing that familiar sour scrunch back to his brow. But this time it was framed in good humor, the way it had been the night before.

He pulled her close and pressed his lips to her forehead. "I guess I haven't."

His chest rose high in a slow, deep breath, and he shifted to get more comfortable, cradling her against him and stretching his long legs out over the edge of the tub. "This has been one helluva day."

"I can't think of a better way to end it."

His sexy moan raked against her ear. "It's not over by a long shot. I'm only resting."

"Don't tell me we've still got unfinished business."

Taking a strand of wet curls between his fingers, he toyed with it. "Something tells me our business will never be finished." Then he smoothed it back behind her ear.

She wondered what he meant by that, but chose to leave the question unspoken. This was just a two-night stand, maybe three if the pawnshop didn't open tomorrow. That constituted a light fling, understood with pure clarity by both of them, agreed with from the onset then reiterated today.

Still, it left an odd sense of connection in her heart, one Georgia's stern warnings had her fearing. So, lifting up from the tub, she pulled herself to her feet and held out a hand. "In that case, I suggest our next business meeting be held somewhere more comfortable. Preferably somewhere dry and cushy."

The sexy gleam came back to his eyes, placing her thoughts where this temporary union belonged—in the throes of good sex.

Really, really good sex.

11

VOICES in the hallway of the busy hotel woke Rick from what had been another restful night. Doors slamming, keys jingling, laughter and conversation echoed through the doorway, and Rick blinked to see the digital readout on the clock beside him.

Nine-thirty. Another record. Two solid nights' sleep in two days, all thanks to the woman beside him.

Or was she?

The familiar scene had him reaching a hand out, half expecting nothing but cold sheet, but this time he ran into the warm body of one hot Texas cowgirl. He smiled and rolled over, spooning her against him under starched sheets that seemed exceptionally comfortable for the standard hotel room.

He chalked it up to rest and good company.

Jessie moaned and turned in his arms, pressing her nose to his chest and then kissing it. She felt good, her soft curls and silky body all snuggled against him, giving him a sense of peace in the cocoon of the small double bed.

Not to mention a hard-on.

He took her hand and guided it down to the stiff shaft between them, and her giggle came out with hot breath against his neck. It had been an unsubtle hint for her to do with it as she wanted, but instead of taking the bait, she slid her hand back to his chest.

"Sorry, Sheriff. We're all out of condoms." She rolled over and drew the blankets up around her shoulders, adding through a yawn, "Room service will be here any minute."

"You ordered condoms from room service?"

She laughed, the fun, pleasant sound making up for one very disappointed cock. "No." Then she stopped and pondered. "Do they do that?"

"I'm sure people have tried."

Her satiny hair tickled his skin when she shook her head. "I called for coffee. I think we missed the free breakfast buffet."

"When did you do that?"

"About fifteen minutes ago."

He pointed to the phone at her side. "From there?"

"No, telepathy. What do you think?"

"I'm just surprised I didn't hear you."

She scooted closer and wiggled her ass against his waist, a very cruel move if they were indeed out of condoms. "You must have been tired."

He'd been tired for nearly three years, but that had never equated to a good night's sleep. Now he'd had two in a row.

He chose not to analyze that and instead questioned this alleged condom shortage. She'd thrown more than a couple on the bed last night and he was hard-pressed to believe they'd gone through all of them.

He pushed up and surveyed the dim room. "We went through all those condoms?"

She turned onto her back, rubbing her sleepy eyes before stretching out like a lazy cat. "A gross underestimation on my part. I'd thought three would have been plenty."

"You bought more than three." He slipped out of the warm bed and began searching the floor, lifting up disheveled clothing, excitedly reaching for a foil packet then deflating when he discovered it empty.

Jessie propped up on the bed, an amused smile on her face as she witnessed his growing desperation. "No. The woman in the gift shop last night looked like she hadn't gotten any since the Korean war. I didn't want to shove my prosperity in her face."

Rick smiled. "She was a little uptight, huh?"

A knock on the door had Jessie slinking back under the covers while Rick slipped on his pants and went to answer it. At least they had coffee, he thought, and after accepting the tray and tipping the server, he poured them two steaming cups and settled in the stuffy chair against the window. Under the circumstances, climbing back into bed was unthinkable.

"I suppose we should see if that pawnshop is open today," he said.

"If it's not, I need to stay another night. I'm not going home without my things if I don't have to." She took a long sip and added, "Couldn't you pull some cop strings and get the guy to open for us?"

"On a slow day, maybe. But you saw this town last night. We're low on the list." Which meant Rick would have to spend another night, as well—an option that wasn't sounding all that bad right now.

Then he remembered he'd turned off his phone last night and went to turn it on. Though slim, there was still a possibility his car could turn up from the APB, and if Wade hadn't checked the trunk, the laptop could still be in it.

Jessie slid out of bed and began straightening her

clothes. She picked up her wrinkled shirts and tried smoothing them over the spare bed. "I'm going to take a shower," she said. "Maybe I can steam some of the creases out of this stuff without dragging out the ironing board."

Grabbing his shirt from the floor, he followed her lead by hanging it on the knob of the bathroom door. It wasn't in bad shape, but if they were staying another night, he figured a trip to a clothing store would be on the agenda today.

After Jess flipped on the shower and disappeared into the bathroom, he checked his phone for messages. There were none, but he called Kevin anyway.

"Fong," Kevin said when he answered.

"It's Rick. Any news?"

"Sorry, partner. Not a peep. If your guy left the Bay Area as quick as we think he did, he's long gone."

"What about Creed? Did the captain do what I'd suggested?"

On a hunch, Rick had urged their captain to confess the laptop had been stolen while in transit to a specialist. The original statement from the force was that it was still with the crime lab, and as expected, Creed's lawyers had erupted with a string of threats. But rather than continue taking the heat, Rick wanted to test their reaction to the knowledge that the laptop was gone, and after expressing his reasoning to the boss, he'd only been told they'd think about it.

"He did."

Rick perked. "And?"

"Just like you suspected. They stopped screaming and backed off."

"Really." Rick wasn't as surprised as he should have been.

"Granted, it's Sunday. Maybe they've taken the day off and will come back when the courts open tomorrow."

"Ten bucks says they won't."

"Twenty bucks says you're right."

Though it was still too premature to be certain, Rick knew in his gut that when tomorrow came around, Creed's lawyers wouldn't be pushing to get that laptop found. Instead they were no doubt promising Creed he had nothing to worry about. The chain of custody had been broken. The evidence was compromised. Now, even if they did find the laptop, nothing anyone uncovered would stand up in a court of law.

And if they did stop screaming to get the precious hardware back, Rick would know for certain he'd been on the right track.

Rick was no idiot. No software developer kept anything of value on a laptop without backup. He'd smelled the rot in that statement the minute he heard it from Creed's lawyers, which was what had sent him after the equipment in the first place. He knew it wasn't software they were after—it was evidence. And the less they fought now that they'd heard it had been stolen, the more certain Rick would be that they wanted it gone, not recovered.

"Keep me posted on that, would you?" He took another swig of his coffee then moved to fill his cup. "One sound from Thornton's lawyers and give me a call. If they start screaming for us to find that laptop, they were probably telling the truth and I can end this wild-goose chase."

"I don't think they will. I'm with you on this one. Things went eerily calm when Captain told them it was stolen. Maybe they're regrouping, but I don't think so. I think if the thing has disappeared, they're fine leaving it that way."

Which made it all the more urgent that Rick got it back.

He needed to know what was on that laptop that Creed was trying to hide. With no other leads on the case, even compromised evidence was better than none at all. It could at least point them to a place they hadn't been looking. And a break in a cold case was a break in a cold case, no matter where it came from.

He said his goodbyes and flipped off the phone just as Jessie stepped from the bathroom. Her cheeks were shiny clean and flush from the heat. Her normally curly hair was weighted straight from the water, darkened to a chocolate-brown that highlighted those honey eyes and reddened her generous lips. A fat, fluffy towel surrounded her like a tortilla, and still hungry for the woman, he ached to uncoil the cloth and taste the treats inside.

"We're out of condoms," she said, obviously reading the look in his eyes. "Of course, that only means intercourse isn't an option." She undraped the towel and let it fall to the ground, and his cock swelled at the sight of that slim body, naked and ripe for the taking.

"I don't know about you," she added, "but I can come up with a few alternatives." Then she eyed the bulge in his pants. "That is, if you're *up* for it."

He dropped the cell phone and moved toward her, kicking off his pants in the process so that by the time he'd taken her in his arms and plopped her on the bed, he was hard, ready and willing.

"Is this what you had in mind?" he asked, parting her thighs and digging his teeth gently into the tender flesh around her thighs.

"Oh, yeah," she groaned.

Then he proved in no uncertain terms he was most definitely *up* for it.

RICK SHOWERED while Jessie checked for phone messages and tried to get in touch with friends or family back home who might have heard from Wade. It was now heading toward noon and they'd yet to make it back to the pawnshop to see if it had opened. They were moving fairly slow this morning, and for the first time in years, it didn't seem to bother him.

"I got hold of my brother Trip," Jessie said over the shower. "I guess Momma and Ray are in Fort Worth for a wedding. They won't be back until tomorrow night."

"You have a brother named Trip?" Rick asked.

"He's my stepbrother. His real name is Trevor. I never asked how he ended up with Trip, now that you mention it. As long as I knew him, he was always just Trip."

He dabbed shampoo in his hand and began lathering his hair. "So, is it a Texas thing that everyone's got a nickname? Where does Sugar come from?"

"My daddy named me that. Momma wanted Jessica, but as the story goes, when I was born, Daddy said I looked sweet as sugar, so they made it official."

Jessie had told him about her childhood during their drive to Nevada. How her father had been killed during an army training mission, and though he'd never served in a war, they'd awarded him the Medal of Commendation and full veteran benefits to his wife and only child.

"So your real name is Sugar Beane?" he asked, working hard to hold the smile from his lips.

"Well, that's up for debate. When Momma married Ray, she wanted to change my name from Hawley to Beane. That was the first feud that erupted between her and my granna."

"You gave me the impression they don't get along."

She laughed. "That's an understatement. Granna Hawley had a fit. I was her only grandchild and Daddy had been her only child. I don't think my name was ever changed officially, but everywhere Momma could, she signed my name Sugar Beane just to spite her. I only changed it to Jessica when I moved to California. The whole starting over thing."

"I like Jessica," he said.

She began to say something but was interrupted by the phone. "It's my friend, Darlene, from Texas," she said, optimism in her voice as he heard her say "Hello" and disappear from the bathroom. He hoped this call would fare well.

It was several minutes later when he shut off the water and as he dried off, he found the room oddly quiet.

Too quiet, his gut said.

Wrapping the towel around his waist, he stepped out to find Jessie sitting on the bed staring at the phone in her hand.

"You all right, babe?"

She looked up at him with glassy eyes. "Yeah. Just another dead end, that's all."

Though she kept her tone steady, he could see by the look on her face there was more to the call than that.

"Was it the friend you were expecting?"

She laughed bitterly as though he'd made a pun. "It was Darlene, all right, but not the person I expected." She tossed the phone in her purse. "She's moved to the dark side, apparently."

"I don't understand." He crossed the room and sat down next to her.

Jessie jutted her chin, though her eyes couldn't hide what was obviously hurt. "Darlene and I have been friends since grade school. She was one of the few who stood by me during my divorce." She blinked back tears and squared her shoulders. "I guess things have changed in the last year. She's hooked up with Sam Reynolds, one of Wade's old pals, and doesn't think it would be a good idea for us to keep in touch."

Rick shook his head, having serious problems understanding the people in this town she came from. "So, what, you're not friends anymore?"

"She was a bridesmaid at my wedding," she said, turning her face to the wall. "Of all the people, her and Georgia—" Standing up quickly, she grabbed her shirt and finished getting dressed. "It doesn't matter."

Rick would've liked to believe that, but it was obvious this person did matter. What wasn't obvious was how an entire town could chastise a woman for divorcing her husband. There had to be something she wasn't telling him.

"I don't understand, Jess. What's with these people? It's the twenty-first century. Couples get divorced all the time."

"Oh, it wasn't the divorce." She pulled the black top over her head and tucked it under her belt. "I helped bring down the town hero."

"A convicted car thief was your town's hero?"

Grabbing her black heeled shoes, she lowered into the chair to put them on. "You have to understand Tulouse. It had been dying ever since the Holstead Equipment Company closed its doors back in the eighties. The company practically employed the whole town, and when they closed, people started moving away in droves. Homes boarded up, stores closed. Only the original farmers were left and their kin, people who didn't want to leave the land that had been in their families for generations.

"It wasn't the happiest place to grow up. By the time I came around, there was a lot of poverty and barely enough kids to keep the high school going. But in Wade's senior year—that was three years ahead of mine—the football team went to State."

She settled back in the chair and smiled wistfully. "You should have seen everyone. Stan Archer, the quarterback, Johnny Lane, the wide receiver, and Wade, their most colorful front lineman, they were all heroes. They put Tulouse back on the map and gave people something to be proud of. To this day, those three are kings of the city, and you can believe everyone looked the other way when they got caught stealing cars."

"Except you."

Her eyes grew dark and angry. "Heroes are supposed to be men like my father who served their country instead of stole from it." She shook her head in disgust. "And no hero would expect his wife to lie to the law in order to save his hide."

"He wanted you to lie to the police?"

"He didn't even have the opportunity to ask. They brought me in for questioning and I told them the truth. I didn't know what else to do. Wade had been arrested. They wouldn't let me talk to him. They asked questions, I answered. Why wouldn't I? I didn't think we had anything to hide. But when he found out I hadn't even tried to cover for him, he turned."

Pain crossed her face as she explained. "People don't know how he reacted. They don't know what he can be like." She leveled those eyes at him. "You ever see the rage some football players conjure up on the field? You ever see that and understand why they're so good at taking men down?"

He knew where she was going and wasn't sure he wanted to hear it.

"That man was no hero. But the more I said so, the less

people wanted to hear it. He was the boy who brought pride back to Tulouse. They weren't going to let a few stolen cars dim the light he shined on the town, and they certainly weren't going to believe their golden child was capable of raising a hand to his wife."

A sour taste filled Rick's mouth. That familiar taste he got too often on the job. It tightened his jaw, curled his hands into fists and gave him one more reason to wish like hell he could find Wade Griggs.

"Don't worry," she said, noting the look in his eyes. "He only got away with it once. I was gone before he could try it a second time."

Hallelujah, he thought, but it did little to uncoil the anger in his gut.

Jess sniffed hard, reared her shoulders back and smiled. "Old history." She rose from the couch and moved for her purse.

He wanted to wrap her in his arms and console away the pain, but as quickly as she'd stood, her eyes had reverted to their usual cheerful state.

"What do you say we drop by the pawnshop then find something to eat?" she asked. "I'm starved."

"We can do anything you'd like."

He'd spoken softly and her brow furrowed. "Don't treat me like a china doll. Darlene was a disappointment, nothing more."

"I'm very sorry for everything you went through."

"It's done and over with." She tossed him his shirt. "Get dressed. If we're stuck in this town, we might as well have some fun."

He stepped to her and cupped her chin in his hand. "You sure you're okay? I know you don't know me well, but you don't have to put up a front." He patted his shoulder. "I've got a strong one if you need something to cry on."

She laughed and kissed his cheek. "Thanks, Sheriff, but if I let stuff like this get me down, the world would have swallowed me up before kindergarten." She shrugged. "What's done is done. I thought Darlene was a friend. Now I know she's not. Nothing I can do about it, so all that's left is to suck it up and move on."

Then she pulled a stick of lip balm from her purse and stepped to the bathroom, leaving him wondering if she was as strong as she appeared.

Suck it up and move on, she'd said.

If he could only believe life was that easy.

12

I THINK IT'S BEST if you don't call here anymore.

Darlene's words played back in Jessie's thoughts, making a sore spot in her chest where their friendship used to be.

You and Georgia are gone, Darlene had tried to explain. *Me and Sam got something going on. You understand, don't you, Sugar? You know how it is around here.*

Yeah, Jessie understood. Almost two years since Wade's arrest and they still wanted to blame her for his demise, as if she'd single-handedly brought him and his shop down. She hadn't. Plenty of people testified against Wade and his buddies. But the difference was everyone else had been from out of town. She'd been one of their own, and in a town like Tulouse, when outsiders come in and try to destroy your heroes you're supposed to stick together no matter what.

Unfortunately that wasn't the example her granna Hawley had set.

Jessie reached for the newspaper that had come with their coffee. "I was looking at this when you were shaving. It's a list of all the events going on today."

She smiled away the pain from Darlene's call, not willing to give more of her heart than had already been taken. For Jessie, that meant focusing her energy on the future, not the past. "Look at the pictures. These Show-N-Shines look fun."

Rick eyed her warily and she knew what he was thinking.

"I'm fine," she assured. "Really." But he didn't respond with words. Instead he stepped close, cupped her face in his palms and studied her eyes. He smiled faintly, his gaze providing sympathy she didn't need, but before she could shrug him off, he leaned in and pressed his mouth to hers.

Where before his kisses had been hot and hungry, these lips were warm and giving, not intended to invoke passion but to console and reassure. He kissed her cheek and hugged her close. Touching her lips again, he held her against him in a way that said more than words could express.

And though her brain warned it was a bad idea, she let her body sink in and take the offering. Truth was, she did hurt, and it wasn't often that she felt such strong, protective arms around her. The moment warmed her blood and touched an empty place inside she hoped to someday fill. Silently, she let the sense of comfort and safety spill through her.

He kissed her gently, brushing a hand over her hair, squeezing away the tension at the back of her neck and caressing sweet condolences down her shoulders and arms. It felt good. So good, she nearly forgot this was a man only offering her physical pleasure.

A man who'd made it clear physical pleasure was all he had to give.

But there was nothing physical going on here. This was a kiss straight from the soul. A sensitive, nurturing side of Rick that was tender and kind and dangerous as hell to the needy side she was trying to overcome. The emotion lodged in her throat and caught her breath, and before she let it find an entrance to her heart, she broke the kiss and stepped back.

His arms drifted from her sides and she patted a casual hand to his chest. "Thank you. I really am fine." Then she took another step back, shoved the newspaper in his hand and filled the awkward moment by adding, "After the pawnshop, let's go to a car show. Are you into cars? All guys are, aren't they?"

Oh, smooth as gravel, Jess.

He held his gaze on hers for a final beat before smiling casually and taking the paper in his hand. "Sure. To tell you the truth, my dad used to own a muscle car. It might be fun to check out."

"Then it's decided." Her voice was shrill and she worked to calm it as she gathered her things. "Let's go have some fun."

AN HOUR LATER they'd confirmed the pawnshop was still closed, had raided a hot-dog stand on the corner of Virginia Street and were now walking off their meal amidst a sea of brightly painted cars, trucks and roadsters. Some had their hoods open to display shiny chrome engines, others kept them down to show off hot painted flames. They passed by an Elvis impersonator, flanked by girls in poodle skirts, on his way toward a stage where fifties music blared from large black speakers. An emcee announced the band as Johnny and the Elmos, and when Rick turned and raised a brow, Jessie erupted in laughter.

"If they're red and fuzzy, we're leaving," Rick quipped, and Jessie laughed again. The sight and sound warmed him. Though she'd tried to put up a front, he could see that the call from home had hurt, and it was nice to hear her spirit returned. After hearing her story, he'd been proud of her for getting out of Texas and moving to San Francisco. It was no doubt a huge culture shock, a move that took guts, and he liked that about her. Jessica Beane was tough, even tougher than him in many ways, but that instance back at the hotel reminded him that she had open wounds that hadn't healed yet.

And if anyone understood those, it was him.

Placing her hand in his, they strolled among rows and rows of cars, each guarded by an owner anxious to talk about his or her pride and joy.

"My dad had an old Plymouth Road Runner," he said. "Lime-green with a big black racing stripe over the hood." He watched two older men holding a conversation over the engine of a '56 Chevy. "That thing could have done two hundred miles an hour." Then he muttered under his breath, "If I'd gotten my hands on it."

"You never got to drive it?"

Rick shook his head. "My mom made him sell it when I was a teenager. She was afraid I'd take it out and kill myself in it."

She scoffed. "You? I can't imagine you getting in trouble for anything."

That had him laughing all over again. "I was a hellion."

"Right. On your own personal scale, maybe." She eyed him over the tops of her sunglasses. "Tell me how you grew up. What did your parents do? You have brothers and sisters?"

"One sister, older, married and living down in Watsonville. My dad was a cop for the SFPD until he retired five years ago. We lived in the Sunset until my sister and I were in elementary school. Then my parents followed all their friends to the burbs. Mom and Dad are still in the house I grew up in, down in San Mateo."

"Sounds pretty Wonder Bread to me."

He bit back any objection, realizing that against the things Jessie told him about her family life, that's exactly what it had been—an average, run-of-the-mill upbringing, where his life tooled along rather effortlessly. From his earliest memories he'd known what he wanted from life, what he was going to be, where he'd live, and from college on, even who he was going to marry. And throughout his life, everything had gone along right as planned.

Until Nat's death.

He shook away the thought, not wanting to go there. For the first time in months, he was happy and he didn't care to self-destruct just yet.

"That doesn't mean I didn't have my moments," he said.

She didn't buy it. "Name one thing you did to get in trouble."

"I wrecked a friend's motorbike flying over a hill trying to catch air up on Crane Mountain Road. Almost killed myself."

"No!"

"Yes. It was the incident that caused them to sell the Road Runner. They weren't about to take any chances."

She grinned. "I'm impressed. Maybe there is a little renegade in you."

They continued walking toward the music, Rick stopping at the occasional Mustang or Camaro, reminiscing over cars his friends had owned. Rehashing those events seemed like a lifetime ago. He didn't often think back to his high school days. Those early times with him and Nat usually stirred up too much pain. But oddly, today, with the music blaring, the sun shining high over this kaleidoscope of colored metal and the murmur of the crowd around them, the memories didn't seem to hurt so much.

"A buddy of mine had one of these old Impalas," he said. "You could hear that thing coming from three miles away."

Jessie laughed, just as he saw it. The chrome front bumper of a Plymouth Road Runner, poking out from a lime-green quarter panel.

"No way." He took her hand and picked up the pace. "Damn if this isn't the same car my dad had."

Jessie trailed behind him. "This is *the* car?"

He looked the car over. "No, but it's almost the spitting image."

Eyeing it sweetly, he ended up introducing himself to the car's owner, Bob McKernan, and his wife, Carla Sue, both having driven here all the way from Tacoma, Washington. Bob was an older man with friendly blue eyes and a gut that said he was well fed. Rick learned he'd made a career as a mechanic for UPS and spent his spare time fixing up muscle cars and selling them for a profit. Carla Sue looked to be his perfect mate with her dyed-red up-do, neatly pressed Mom jeans and a shirt that said Trophy Wife in studded pink rhinestones.

The four spent the next hour getting to know each other, Bob and Rick talking cars while Carla Sue gave Jessie the rundown on their daughter and two sons, the oldest a Marine and stationed in Iraq. And before he knew it, Rick found himself behind the wheel of the car, gripping the steering wheel and feeling the heat of the black vinyl seat against his back.

As a kid he'd spent hours sitting in his dad's, pretending he was Steve McQueen or Clint Eastwood flying down the streets of San Francisco.

"It's for sale," Jessie said, sliding into the long bench seat behind him.

He smoothed his hand over the wood laminate console between the front bucket seats, soaked in the smell of dust, gas and oil, and smiled fondly at the "Beep Beep!" Warner Brothers character that gave the car its name.

"Every year I bring a car down to sell," Bob added, grinning from under the rim of his Shamrock University baseball cap.

"I'm not in the market for a car today," Rick said, and in the rearview mirror, he caught Jessie's scowl.

"I'm not," he insisted.

"No one's in the market for a car like this," Jessie argued. "This is something you buy on impulse, for fun, to live a little." Then she eyed Carla Sue, who had slid in beside her. "You know, after you go for a test drive and can't live without it."

"Show's almost over and we don't have any plans until the all-you-can-eat buffet back at Silver Legacy tonight," Carla said.

Bob stepped away from the driver's-side window, dropped the hood with a thud and took the passenger seat next to Rick. "She's a beauty." He ran a hand over the black vinyl dash. "All original. The floorboards have been redone, but the upholstery's factory. They just don't come this clean anymore."

Rick was getting the hard sell from all angles, Jessie egging them on and giving the poor couple hope. But damned if he wasn't enjoying it. He hadn't so much as thought about this old car in years, much less fantasized about someday owning one.

Jessie winked at Carla Sue. "Personally I think since your dad sold his car because of you, it's your obligation as a good son to buy him a new one now that you're grown and responsible."

He caught her smile in the rearview mirror. "You want me to buy this car for my dad?"

"Why not?"

"I'll give you a good deal," Bob said. "Call it the Father's Day special."

His father would never expect something like this. Not in a million years. And the man's birthday wasn't far off. Rick could clearly see pulling into the driveway and shocking the socks off the old guy.

It was a great idea. Crazy, but great.

Jessie slapped a hand to Bob's shoulder. "He's thinking about it, Bob. Reel him in."

And the next thing Rick knew, he was peeling onto I-80 with his foot on the gas and the wind at his back, having the time of his life with a funky old couple from Tacoma and a sexy redhead who kept turning his life upside down.

IT WAS AFTER 10:00 p.m. before Jessie and Rick made it back to the hotel room, having snagged two extra tickets to the Silver Legacy's all-you-can-eat buffet then dancing off the dinner at a Tribute to Neil Diamond concert at Circus Circus. It was exactly the kind of day Jessie needed to take her mind off her problems with Wade, knowing that tomorrow morning, life was going to come crashing down around her. The pawnshop would open, ending the burning question of whether or not she'd be able to recover Georgia's ring. Hopefully, her lawyer would now be in the office, answering her messages and resolving the question of her divorce.

It was going to either be a good day or a bad day, topped off by an inevitable trip home where she would say goodbye to her weekend lover for good.

The thought brought her a mix of sadness and relief. Though the sex had been great from the start, she'd just gotten a taste of Rick's better side, one she could grow fond of if it lasted. She was on that dangerous ground Georgia warned of, that place where her life's dream of finding Mr. Wonderful shrouded her judgment and turned a blind eye to reality. It had been that same giddy state that had her ignoring the signs that Wade Griggs wasn't the man she thought he was. That Byron Davies before him wasn't the two-timer he'd ended up being. And more pertinent to the moment, that Rick Marshall might change his tune about commitment and want to explore a future with her.

She stood and watched as he pulled tags off the jeans and T-shirts they'd bought at the Hard Rock Cafe before returning to the hotel. Everything about him filled her ideals of the hero she'd always dreamed of. She loved the way he carried himself. He had the ease of a man comfortable in his own skin. An aura of authority surrounded him, as if his badge were somehow always on display and those smart, determined eyes perpetually sizing up his surroundings.

He fit the vague, distant memories she'd had of her father, the ones her grandmother kept alive and glorified with every year that passed. The ones that always got her into trouble, hope and fantasy coloring her reality, making her blind to the obvious.

Rick had told her from the start then repeated often enough that he wasn't in the market for love. It didn't get more obvious than that, which meant she needed to go home, and fast, before her emotions slipped from her control.

"You need to buy that car," she insisted, yanking her thoughts over to a topic easier to deal with.

"I'll think about it," was all he said.

"By the time you get around to deciding, it'll be gone."

"If it's meant to be, it will be."

"Spoken like a man too chicken to take the chance."

He dropped the clothes on the table and took her in his arms, gyrating his hips against hers. "I wasn't too chicken to dance with you tonight."

He spun her around and she laughed. "And lo and behold, you're a pretty good dancer," she said.

Then he unclipped her belt, letting it fall to the ground before pulling her shirt up over her head. "And I'm pretty good at a few more things, too."

She grabbed for his fly. "Really? It's been so long, I forget now."

"Then let me remind you."

It took only a moment before they were naked on the bed, her body sprawled under his and his hard cock pressed against her waist. And tonight, it only took a moment to notice that the tone had changed. Where before he'd been a hot and fiery lover, this time he was tender and calm. Those once slick moves geared to lifting her high and dropping her hard had mellowed into something sensual. And as he moved his body over hers, she felt the shifting tide that had started this morning and carried on through the day.

He fluttered light kisses down her shoulder, across her breasts, around her waist and between her legs, each one bringing slow and tempered warmth deep inside her core. He worked her without fury, using a slow burn instead, building and ebbing, tasting and caressing until her body hummed in a low, even beat.

In another time, he'd send her crashing, bringing release swift and thorough. Or he'd teasingly pull back, not willing to let her boil over until she'd begged and ached and sobbed. Both options had been joyous, exactly the kind of sex she'd sought out for this purely physical tryst. But tonight, instead of thrusting her over the edge, he kept the slow tempo going by slipping inside.

He evened his gaze with hers, tender affection darkening those sizzling blues as his body filled hers, taking her deep and stroking her slow while he kissed her gently and joined in the gradual build. They moved together in a blending of body and soul, sensation coursing through her with every sweet press of his mouth to hers. His heady gaze consumed her as it shifted from giving to needy to greed, her breath hitching when they both hit the peak and the moment neared.

And when she crossed, he bent in and covered her mouth with his, drinking in her cries, soaking the air from her lungs. Spilling himself inside her, they passed together, joining in motion and spirit like they'd never done before. It came quiet and sensual, more felt than spoken, and when they calmed he spooned her against him, holding her close before stirring up the energy to start again.

And when he'd filled her one last time, she lay against him, his warm breath wafting across her bare shoulder as she studied the dark shadows of the quiet hotel room. She loved being cocooned in the arms of the protector she'd always wanted. It was then she realized the fantasy had taken over. She'd transformed her sexy plaything into the dark hero of her dreams, and now she stood in quicksand, only time between her and another fateful heartache.

She hoped that tomorrow she'd find Georgia's ring so

she could end this affair, recognizing full well that she was seeing and feeling and believing in things that had no basis in reality.

This had been easier yesterday, back when Rick was a safe, teasing, hot and fiery cop. The guy who would hate her if their bodies hadn't meshed so well, the grouchy grump who was angry at the world, angry with her, and more trouble than he was worth.

She'd been on even ground with that one. He'd been easy to deal with and easier to leave. But now he was gone, replaced by a gentle soul that threatened to take her heart and shred it.

Staring at the ceiling, Georgia's warnings echoed in her ears, and this time she didn't scoff at them. This time she knew Georgia was right.

She needed to get her things and go home.

13

"I FOUND IT, Georgia. The pawnshop had your ring."

Jessie stood on the busy sidewalk, nearly bursting at the seams. "They have Grandpa's watch and just about everything else Wade took from the apartment."

"*Just* about?" Georgia asked. "What's still missing?"

Her joy dampened, but only slightly. "Daddy's medal wasn't there. The pawnshop owner said it hadn't been worth anything. Rick's in there right now arranging for a copy of the police report to be faxed over. He said it may take a few days for us to get our things, but we'll get them. They're being officially seized as stolen property."

"That's awesome, Jess."

It was, and after three days of anxiety, waiting through the weekend for the shop to open, Jessie finally felt her first wave of relief. With Georgia apparently her only friend left from back home, she really didn't want the loss of the ring between them, no matter how many times Georgia claimed it wasn't Jessie's fault.

"So it's back to San Francisco?"

"Yes. I'll either be coming back with Rick or hopping on a bus. I'm not sure what he's doing. We never found Wade, and Rick's car still hasn't turned up. He's been great helping me get my things from the pawnshop."

"That's mighty kind of him," Georgia droned. She still hadn't forgiven Rick for the way he'd stormed into Hidden Gems and accused Jessie of being a car thief.

"It was, and you'll be happy to know our weekend tryst is done and over and that I've made it to Monday without the slightest crack in my heart."

And in a few days, she'd actually believe that. For now, she had to admit that a tiny little side of her—a tiny, irrational side—had sorta maybe fallen for the guy.

Of course, she'd never admit that to Georgia. Georgia, already soured on love as it was, would never understand how an intelligent woman could lose her heart to a man after only knowing him two days. And Jessie wouldn't have an argument for her. She couldn't rationalize chemistry. She could only explain how she felt, and after spending two days with the man, she couldn't ignore the sizzle up her spine or the light fluttery feeling in her stomach whenever he was around.

Still, even if Georgia's warnings didn't give her pause, Rick himself had been clear that he wasn't in the market for a relationship. So now was a good time to cash in her chips while she was still ahead.

"I'm proud of you," Georgia said. "Maybe your year off men taught you something, after all."

Jessie peered through the window and saw that Rick was still caught in conversations between his cell phone and the pawnshop owner.

"It hadn't taught me enough. I haven't been able to get hold of my lawyer yet about the divorce. I keep getting the answering machine." And she didn't *even* want to talk to Georgia about Darlene, deciding today would be a day about good news, not bad.

"Lots of offices are closed on Mondays. Don't worry about that. You'll straighten it out when you're home."

"Rick's still questioning the pawnshop owner, but I'll be see you later today, I'm sure."

"Cool, then we'll have dinner tonight. You can tell me all about your adventures."

Jessie said her goodbyes and shut off the phone before stepping into the pawnshop.

"I already told you," the shop owner insisted. "The guy didn't say nuthin' about a laptop. I wouldn't have taken it anyway. We don't take computers here."

The grim frown had returned to Rick's face, the one she hadn't seen since the day before yesterday. She wouldn't mind trying to transform it into a smile, but then stopped herself, remembering that was no way to think about a temporary fling.

"What's this about a laptop?" she asked as she approached the counter.

"It was in my car," Rick said. "I was hoping Wade had pawned it."

The smile drained from her face. "I'm sorry. I didn't know. Did you have your files backed-up?"

He flicked his phone closed then opened it again and dialed another number. "It wasn't my laptop. It was evidence in a case." Then he held up a finger and spoke to the phone. "Kevin, what do you have for me?"

Jessie stood watching him talk as a dozen pieces to the puzzle clicked into place. And when they did, a hot flush of dismay sped over her.

She'd been so wrapped up in her own problems and her lust for the sexy cop, she hadn't even wondered why Rick had been so adamant about getting his car back. She'd assumed it was typical male pride, or maybe a typical cop's reaction to wanting to catch a crook. But now it was obvious. It wasn't Wade or his car he wanted back, it was what had been inside.

While he talked to his partner, she rewound the last three days, back to their initial conversation at the bar, minor chitchat about what he did and a case he was working on. She remembered the couple at the station, asking about their murdered daughter.

And then it hit her.

That's what I was about to find out before your husband stole my car.

She'd asked about the couple, those poor distraught people. Had questioned Rick about who murdered their daughter.

He flicked off the phone and turned back to the shop owner, providing the man with his business card then taking one in return. "They'll be faxing you the order this afternoon. If there are any problems, call me."

Then he turned to Jessie.

"The laptop. That had to do with the couple back at the station the other day," she said.

He took her arm and led her out the door. "It did."

Panic crept through her. "Is their daughter's killer going to go free because Wade stole your car?"

"Possibly."

Her stomach turned and her fingers began to shake. She'd been so focused on Georgia's ring and their jewelry and her father's medal and the divorce and Wade's threats. The whole time, she'd only been thinking of herself. And now all those things seemed so trivial and petty.

Her feet stopped moving, causing him to stop. "I'm so sorry." The words felt tight in her throat.

"It's not your fault."

"What was on that laptop? E-mails or receipts or financials?"

When he caught the look in her face, he came close and placed a warm hand on her shoulder. "Jess, the crime lab hadn't found anything. I'd just been transporting it to someone else to see if he could find something." Then he squeezed her shoulder in a gesture of comfort. "There might have been nothing on that laptop. It was probably a dead end."

"If you were sure about that, you wouldn't have driven all the way here to find it."

Acknowledgment flashed in his eyes, but he was too much of a gentleman to say so. "It's the way I am, Jess. Don't take responsibility for this."

Now tears welled in her eyes, not only because she felt horrible, but because he was so sweetly trying to make her feel better. Where her ex-husband slapped her hard for not lying to the police, this gentle man was trying to stop her from blaming herself for botching an entire investigation.

"I need to sit down," she whispered, her knees weak and her stomach churning. "Why didn't you tell me this from the start?"

"It's not your concern."

"Like hell. I'm the reason Wade showed up at your place Friday night."

"You're not responsible for your husband's actions."

"Ex," she countered, but there wasn't much heat behind it. The way she felt right now, neither husband nor ex-husband fit the bill as nicely as *dead* husband would, and as the shock began to wear off, bitter anger took its place.

Wrapping an arm around her shoulder, he led her two blocks up and over to a café that looked busy but not swamped. There Rick proceeded to tell her about Paolo and Lucy Mendoza, their daughter, Anna, and the circumstances around her death.

Jessie sipped the ginger ale she'd ordered while she listened to the tragic story, and the more she heard, the more determined she was to help track down Wade.

"This Creed guy," she said. "You think he killed her, don't you? Set it up so that it looked like a suicide?"

"I only think what the evidence tells me."

She raised a brow. That was a practiced line if she'd ever heard one.

She tried a different angle. "What do you think the evidence on that laptop will tell you? Do you think he paid someone to kill her?"

"There are a number of theories and I wouldn't rule out either of those. I'm only going on a hunch that there's something on that laptop he doesn't want the police to see. It could have nothing to do with Anna's murder at all." He shrugged and sipped his black coffee. "Maybe the guy's cheating on his taxes and thinks I care."

"Or maybe it's the proof you need to support one of your theories."

His only response was a faint twitch to his eye as he took another sip from his cup. And that was fine. Jessie had heard enough. Reaching into her purse, she pulled out her phone and address book, flipped through the pages then dialed the number.

"Hello?"

"Cynthia, it's Sugar. I need to—"

"*Sugar?*"

"Yes, Cynthia—"

"You've got a lot of nerve calling here. It's bad enough you've ruined my son's life, *and* now you've broken his heart. What are you doing, Sugar, calling up to finish the job?"

"Broken Wade's heart? I don't understand."

"Oh, we know what you did. It's all over town."

"What's all over town? Cynthia, I was calling to—"

"How do you think he felt spending all that time in jail *for you,* only to find you in bed with another man? What do you think that did to him?"

Jessie's pulse began to speed. "You've talked to Wade?"

"He told us you two weren't divorced and about the happy reunion he had planned. I said to him he was crazy even talking to you after what you did, but he wanted to go anyway. Well, now he knows what we've all been telling him for months. Except now you aren't just a gold digger, you're an adulterer!"

"Cynthia, I'm not—"

"You're a slut! A horny, lousy sl—"

Jessie snapped the phone shut and stiffened her upper lip. "That was a mistake."

Rick placed a hand over hers. "You okay? You're pale. Who was that?"

"Wade's mother." Jessie shook her head. "She wasn't making any sense." Then she swallowed and dialed another number.

"Jess, you don't have to do this."

"Yello."

"Trip, it's me. I just talked to Cynthia Griggs."

"You what?" Her stepbrother laughed. "You got a death wish? That woman's all fired up to tan your ass after Wade called home."

"Wade called?" She met Rick's stare. "Where is he, Trip?"

"Hell if I know. All I know is Cynthia went to church last night cryin' all kinds of things about you. Said Wade went looking for you, hoping to reconcile, wanting to put his marriage back together even after what you did, only to find you screwing some other guy. What you doin' out there, Sugar?"

"Trip, you know me and Wade are divorced. It's been over for—"

"Not the way he's talking. He's got this whole town riled up all over again. Your momma's not going to like this." She heard a noise. He'd upped the volume on the television. "I'm gonna have to get the hell out of here before she and Dad get home. All that yellin'."

"Trip, Wade robbed me and Georgia, then stole a car!"

"Heartsick over you, no doubt."

"Oh, for crying out loud." Now she was just getting mad. "Trip, I need you to find out where he is."

"What's in it for me?"

She clenched her teeth. It was a typical response she should have expected. Ray Beane's boys didn't fall far from the tree, and Jessie hadn't gotten along with any of them since she was a child.

"What do you want, Trip, money? I haven't got any. Maybe for once in your life, you could act like a brother and help me out of the kindness of your heart."

Trip simply laughed.

"Please. It's important."

"Commercial's over. I gotta go. If I hear from Wade, I'll call you."

"Do you have my number?" she attempted, then realized she was talking to a dead phone. "Oh, God."

Rick took the phone from her hand. "Stop with it, Jess. We've already got a call into Wade's parole officer. I'm hoping to hear back soon."

"He's got everyone so snowed." She sipped her soda, now wishing it was something stronger. "He made it out like he came to get me, to make our marriage right."

"Did he?"

Jessie gave him a look. "He came to get the money Granna left me. This is the story he's telling to ward off any accusations I might have." She shook her head and wondered how the man always managed to stay two steps ahead of her.

"The man should have been a carnival barker the way he works a crowd." She shook her head. "This whole thing, this whole story…once he'd seen me again was all about getting to everyone first before I had a chance to explain what really went on. And now everyone's mind is made up. I've got the deck stacked against me from the start, just like two years ago when he was arrested."

Rick studied the coffee cup in his hand. "So he's told everyone he went out to California to reconcile with you."

She nodded and he began to speak again before being interrupted by his cell phone.

He flipped it open. "Marshall." Jessie watched as he listened, nodded, then said, "Good, that's good." Then he hung up. "That was my partner. He got in touch with Wade's parole officer. Apparently he's supposed to check in Thursday, in person. If he doesn't, they'll put a warrant out for his arrest."

"You think Wade's heading for Tulouse?"

"If he's the kind of guy you say he is, he wants to keep the tide turned in his favor. Missing that parole meeting would be a bad move."

Jessie felt green around the gills. The last thing she wanted to do was deal with Wade again, succeeded only by the idea of walking back into Tulouse and facing everyone. But if she didn't, then Wade would win, and she'd simply disappear to California as the adulterous ex-wife of the town's favorite son.

Granna had taught her better than that. Granna had also taught her to take responsibility for her actions, which meant helping Rick get his laptop back. Since she still didn't buy his line that this wasn't her fault. It was. And she couldn't live with herself if she didn't try making this right.

"I think we need to get our hands on a map," Rick said, causing Jessie to glance up to those steady, determined eyes. Even sick to her stomach, the sight of him sparked the blood in her veins, which brought up one last issue.

She could handle facing everyone back home, but could she handle another night with Rick Marshall?

14

A DAY LATER Rick and Jessie were crossing the city limits into Tulouse, Texas, population 984 give or take one sexy redhead. Rick still wasn't sure what he was doing here. The odds were ridiculously slim that Wade would have driven the Dodge Charger all the way here. Even the stupidest criminals wouldn't come rolling into town in a stolen car with out-of-state plates after just being released from jail. And that was given the fact that Rick had come across some pretty stupid criminals in his day.

In this case, he was barely accepting that as a chance. Instead he hoped to get out of Wade where the car was, and if that didn't work, he'd at least walk away having confronted the creep and go home knowing he'd done everything humanly possible to get his evidence back.

Through nearly thirty hours of driving, he'd flashed Wade's picture everywhere and left word with the police and highway patrol where to call if his car turned up. Short of sending out sniffing hounds, he couldn't have done more, which was a small but notable consolation he'd need when he got home and had to face Paolo and Lucy Mendoza again.

He brought his speed down to the posted limit as they rolled into the center of town, which was basically a four-block stretch of highway lined with century-old brick buildings. Not that Rick knew much about architecture. He'd simply noted the placards from the original businesses.

Patwanee & Sons, Est. 1916, one read. Ferguson Hardware, said another, each letter eternally chiseled into the stone of the two-story facades. An old Rialto Theater stood weathered and weary even though the marquee listed two newly released films. Though tired, the town didn't look as grim as Jessie had described, at least, not until they'd passed the main drag and turned onto the backstreets.

"That way," Jessie said, instructing him to take a left at an abandoned strip mall. Only ghosts of the original signs topped the storefronts, even the For Lease signs curling and faded from time. The farther they ventured from the center of town, the more Rick saw of the once thriving city that had been crippled by the loss of its largest employer.

To their right, a vacant gas station had succumbed to the local vegetation, high weeds having broken through the cement, their vines circling up the light posts on their way to shattered bulbs. It stood across the street from the library, a clean, well-tended brick building surrounded by a lush manicured lawn. The whole town seemed to be an odd mix of a well-tended present dotted with the sorry remnants of a once-booming past.

"Turn down Plano Way," Jessie said, pointing toward a corner, which seemed to be the threshold between the urban square and its rural surroundings. Acres of green fields spanned ahead of them, the only sign of civilization beyond the turn being a long row of rusted mailboxes and faded yellow newspaper cubbies marked *Herald*.

"What's that way?" he asked.

"I'm guessing Wade's at his momma's house. We lost ours

when he went to jail and I doubt he has enough money to get something new. If he's not there, I've got a couple of other ideas where he might be, all of them on this side of town."

Jessie was fidgeting with the beads on her purse. Rick had learned by observation that was a sign of nerves. "I'm not confronting Wade, if that's got you worried. We'll play this by the book."

"What do you mean?"

"Scope out the neighborhood, eliminate the off chance that I might run into my car, but after that, we're heading for the police station." He patted a hand to her thigh. "I know better than to start knocking on doors outside my jurisdiction."

That seemed to ease her fretting as she perked up and let the strap fall from her fingers. "In that case, take a right up at that gravel road. We can circle around the back and hit all the houses in one loop."

He did, and after a half hour of driving, he'd seen most of Tulouse, lots of it consisting of sparsely populated farms, and none of it containing his missing Dodge Charger. They circled toward town, Rick following Jessie's directions to the center of town. The police station sat a block off Main Street across from an old stone building marked Colbrook County Medical Center. Kitty corner from that stood an abandoned garage, the sign Griggs Automotive still hanging over the boarded windows.

"Wade operated a chop shop across the street from the police station?" Rick asked, not quite believing the level of gonads that must have taken.

"That would be one reason Captain Stott hadn't been too helpful when the county came in and broke the place up. The sheriff's department had made the local police look like a bunch of Keystone Cops."

"And who are they blaming for that?"

It was an educated guess a situation like that didn't occur without repercussions, and Jessie's glare said there were plenty.

"There's some bad blood between the city and county for sure."

"And where did you land?"

"I didn't come out on the good side of either," she said. "At home, I was a traitor. With the county, I was a suspect."

Rick selfishly wondered if he'd get further with the police if he dropped Jessie off at her mother's house first. Until it sunk in how much courage it must be taking her to come back here. The thought hit him hard, and he quickly pulled into a space and turned off the engine.

"What are we going to get when we walk in there?" He pointed at the police station. Now he was wondering for her behalf, not his.

She pursed her brow. "What do you mean?"

"Am I taking you to the wolves?"

Now the furrow in her brow shifted from confusion to defiance. "I'm not afraid of these people."

"I don't think you are, but if it's as bad as you say, you don't need to go face them if you don't want to. I can handle this myself."

She shook her head and set her jaw and he held back a smile. Damn, she was sexy when those eyes filled with fire.

"I'm the reason you've had to come all this way," she said. "If it were up to me, I would have been pounding on Wade's door by now."

He didn't doubt she would have, even though he knew a side she tried to hide would have been scared senseless.

"You want to play it your way and talk to Captain Stott

first, that's your call," she said. "But I'm not running from any of these people. Wade's got some explaining to do and I intend to hear it."

Rick sat for a moment, looking her over and fighting off a flurry of impressions and desires he had no business feeling. Respect for standing up for her values, admiration for leaving everything she knew to start her life over and pride in overcoming her fears when faced with opposition. They all kept sneaking up on him when he had his guard down, warming a spot in his heart he'd thought had frozen over for good. Unfortunately now wasn't the time to map out all the ways she'd crept under his skin, much less consider what he was going to do about it. Besides, this affection could be nothing more than a byproduct of circumstance. They'd spent too much time in too close proximity with too many problems to contend with. Life wasn't normal right now, and the time definitely wasn't ripe for doing or saying anything that could come back to haunt him.

So he shoved it all down by smiling and patting her thigh. "Then let's go."

A HALF HOUR LATER they were standing in the office of Captain Merle Stott, acting chief of the Tulouse city police department, which was a squad consisting of him and three patrolmen. It seemed most everything beyond traffic tickets and basic drunk and disorderlies tended to get taken over by the Colbrook County sheriff's department—a definite sore spot with the captain, as Jessie had warned.

And also as she'd expected, he wasn't thrilled to see her, even less so when he discovered that she'd shown up with a San Francisco homicide inspector intent on accusing Wade Griggs of yet another crime.

"Things got quiet around here after you went off to California," Stott said. The heavy, balding man took a seat behind his desk and gestured for Rick and Jessie to take the two in front of it. "Kinda nice, if you don't mind me saying so."

She let the remark slide, though Rick noted by the look in her eyes that it hadn't been without effort.

"How long do you plan on staying?"

"As long as I care to, Merle." She curled her lip. "You recall I wasn't the Griggs that went to jail."

He shook his head. "No, you weren't," he said in a tone suggesting there was injustice in that.

"Captain Stott," Rick interjected, feeling the need to get between them. "Like I told Officer Leal, I'm here to question Wade Griggs about a car theft. I have evidence to support he may be involved."

"And what kind of evidence is that?"

Rick proceeded to give the captain a few facts, opting to keep the details to a minimum given the obvious bias in the man's tone. Rick had only started here as a courtesy to the police force, but the more he got to know Tulouse's finest, the more he regretted not going straight to Wade like Jessie had wanted.

And when he felt he'd revealed enough, he waited as Stott responded with a skeptical eye. "Seems a long ways to come just to question a man about a stolen car. I would have thought a big-city cop like yourself would have more important cases to solve." And with a grin coated in sarcasm, he added, "We do have telephones here in Texas. You could have called."

"There were valuables in the car that make the recovery of the vehicle a high priority for the San Francisco Police Department."

For the first time since they sat down, Stott pulled a pen from the Texas Longhorn coffee mug he used as a holder and grabbed a pad of paper. "What kind of valuables?"

"A laptop containing information pertinent to a murder investigation."

Stott eyed Rick then turned his gaze to Jessie. "And you're just along for the ride."

It wasn't posed as a question, but Jessie squared her shoulders and answered anyway, taking Rick's lead in saying as little as possible. "That's the sum of it."

Stott blew out a breath and tossed the pen on the pad without having written anything down, then leaned back in his gray vinyl chair. The motion pulled the shirt around his gut so tightly Rick feared a button would go flying and hit one of them square in the eye.

"You seem to be making a career out of putting your husband in jail," he said.

"*Ex*-husband, and if the man would stop breaking the law, I wouldn't have to, now would I?"

He frowned. "That's your accusation. Nothing's been proven as far as I'm concerned."

Her jaw dropped, prompting Rick to step in. He'd seen that look of fire before and didn't want this conversation to fall further in the tank than it already had.

"I'd like to question Mr. Griggs now." He rose from his seat, but Captain Stott waved his stubby fingers, motioning him to sit back down.

"I'll call Wade right now and see what he has to say about all this. If it's necessary, I'll ask him to come down pronto."

He picked up the phone and dialed the number, Rick noting the fact that Stott hadn't needed to look it up. And twenty minutes later, they were still sitting there, listening to one half of a conversation that sounded more like two friends catching up on the latest news than an interrogation. Any moment now, Rick expected Stott to invite Wade up for dinner with the missus as consolation for having to bother him on such a fine day. And as Rick eyed Jessie sitting next to him, the steam coming from her gaze seemed to percolate with every word.

"Yup, I hear you," the captain said, nodding and tapping his pen on the blotter of his large oak desk. He still hadn't taken a note, and Rick guessed it wasn't because the man had a photographic memory.

Stott turned his gaze to Jessie. "Oh, yeah, I understand where you're coming from." Then he eyed Rick and lowered his brow. "No, I don't think that's such a good idea. You let me handle things." Another pause as the faint voice from the receiver seemed to escalate. "Now don't go doing that. This sounds like a simple misunderstanding that I'll have straightened out in no time."

And if Rick had doubted the sense of this meeting before, he knew for certain from that comment he'd just wasted an hour of his life.

Jessie's hands were fisted to the chair, no doubt in an effort to keep from bounding over the desk and strangling the man with the telephone cord. And if she did, Rick had to admit, he'd take his time stopping her. He'd obviously stepped into the middle of the good-old-boy's club, and though Jessie had attempted to warn him, he hadn't quite gotten it until now.

They weren't making any progress here, and he'd just spent four days on the road for the same result.

Finally hanging up the phone, the captain regarded Rick. "Wade admits being in San Francisco." Then he turned a dark eye to Jessie. "He'd come to surprise his wife with the news that he'd been released from jail."

Jessie let out an exasperated gasp. "When will it sink in with everyone that we're divorced?"

"I'm sure that was the first thing on Wade's mind after going all that way and finding you in bed with another man." He pointed a stern eye at Rick. "And since it was your house where you claim to have found Wade's prints, I'm assuming *you're* the other man."

Now Rick's pulse was beginning to match the speed of Jessie's. "He stole my car. I need it back."

Stott held up a hand. "Wade didn't know anything about your car. He said he'd gone into the house believing it was his wife's then ran out after discovering the two of you—" He pressed his lips into a line. "Personally I find it mighty honorable that he turned and came home. Most men I know would have come back with a shotgun, yours truly included."

Jessie shot up from the chair. "The snake is lying through his teeth. He came to California to extort money from me. He threatened me, stole from me and my roommate, then drove out of town with Rick's car. And if you believe anything different, you're as dumb as Sheriff Chaney says you are."

Rick had no idea who Sheriff Chaney was, but he could see by the flash of red that swept over Stott's cheeks the comment had been a low blow.

The man rose from his chair and held out a stern finger, and Rick rose, as well, holding up a hand to halt whatever the man was about to say.

"I'd like to question Mr. Griggs now."

Stott's fiery expression fixed on Rick. "No one's questioning Wade. I've already taken his statement. He didn't steal your car and has a valid explanation for why his fin-gerprints were in your house. Now unless you've got a judge's order to extradite him back to your jurisdiction, I think your business is done here."

"I don't think so. My questions haven't been answered. Besides, I'm sure his parole officer would like to know he's crossed state lines. That can't be part of the agreement."

The captain straightened. "Is that supposed to be some kind of a threat?"

"I didn't drive fifteen hundred miles to listen to your phone conversation. I'm not leaving town until I've spoken to Wade."

Stott stood and eyed them both, his face flushed and his chest huffing from a heart beating too fast for his lungs. "And if he so much as whispers the notion that you're ha-rassing him, I won't stop and think about throwing your ass in jail." Then he turned to Jessie. "You want my advice, you should take your boyfriend and go back to California."

"I don't want your advice," Jessie said coolly. "I want my *ex*-husband to leave me and my friends alone."

Rick placed a hand at the base of her spine and nudged her toward the door. "Captain Stott, it's been a pleasure."

They made it all the way outside without another word from Stott, the hot sun hitting Rick hard like a thick, humid blanket. But barely three steps from the building, he heard the rush of footsteps along with the angry wail, "So you're the son of a bitch been banging my wife!"

Before Rick could turn around completely he was cold-cocked square in the jaw.

Jessie shrieked.

His chin smarted and he instinctively touched a finger

to the corner of his mouth, testing for blood. He felt a hand grab on to the back of his shirt. He was being yanked backward and Jessie lurched toward them when his training kicked in and he shot an elbow back then spun on his heels.

Within a blink he'd backed the man against the brick building and was holding a forearm across his throat.

"You must be Wade," he said, his voice breathless from the shock and the sting to his jaw.

The man struggled so Rick pressed harder, nearly cutting off Wade's airway before he held steady. The man wasn't what he'd expected. The mug shot he'd received off their database had made him look thinner than he was. Though Jessie had told him Wade was a lineman, he still hadn't expected the bulk. The man had steely-green eyes, dirty blond hair and a day-old beard that scratched against the back of Rick's hand, and though his glare was angry, that was quickly changing.

"I could kill you, you filthy bastard," Wade said.

Rick pressed harder against Wade's throat. "You can tell me where my car is."

"I already told Merle, I don't know what you're talking about."

"Yeah, I figured you'd be a little forgetful, so how about we cut a deal? You tell me where my car is, and my memory will go a little foggy, too. Or, you can keep playing dumb and I'll tell your parole officer what you've been doing between visits."

The brief calculation in Wade's eyes confirmed everything Rick already knew. The punk had stolen his car. Now it was just a matter of getting him to talk.

"I don't cut deals with pricks who sleep with other men's wives."

"And I don't call punks who use their wives as punching bags men."

A quick flash of recognition passed over Wade's face. It raised the temperature of Rick's blood another ten degrees and made it harder to hold back. It would be so easy right now to amp up the pressure on this creep's jugular and strangle the life out of him. He'd be doing the world a huge favor.

Unfortunately, before he had a chance to talk himself out of it, he heard Jessie call out an objection right as two pairs of hands grabbed his shoulders and pulled him back. It was Captain Stott and his sidekicks, Gomer Pile and Barney Fife.

The moment they pulled him off, Wade grabbed at his throat and began an overexaggerated fit of wheezing.

"Wade, you all right?" one of them asked.

"He tried to kill me," he choked through a cough.

"This is your last chance to tell me where my car is," Rick said, shrugging off Stott's patrol officers.

"You've got nothing on me. I came back to Texas on a Greyhound bus. Tom Hubley picked me up at the station in Banks and will testify he saw me get off the bus. I've got the ticket to prove it."

"That's enough," Stott growled. He pulled Rick toward his car. "You two go back to where you came from or I'll haul you in for assault."

Rick found it interesting the man wasn't doing that already, but he'd stirred up enough trouble for one afternoon. It was time to find a hotel—maybe in a neighboring town— and regroup now that he knew what he was up against.

"We aren't done," Wade shouted. "That's my wife." The display prompted Rick to go the extra mile and place a possessive hand on Jessie's back as he helped her into the car.

It was a cheap shot, but he did it anyway.

"Yes, you are done," Stott said. "Everyone's going home. You deal with your domestic problems between your lawyers."

It was the only intelligent thing Rick had heard Stott say all day, and as he rounded the car and opened his door, he tossed one last comment to the captain.

"Maybe you should find yourselves a better class of hero."

15

"I'M SORRY." Jessie stared at the road ahead as Rick pulled from the curb and headed down the street. "I'm so sorry about all of this."

"It's not your fault."

His words sounded sincere, and she'd surely like to believe them, but it was hard to forget that none of this would have happened if it hadn't been for her. If she and Rick hadn't met Friday night—if she hadn't all but seduced him in that bar—he might be holding a warrant in his hands, ready to arrest a murderer instead of driving through this dustbowl town getting a front-seat view of the ignorant swill she came from.

After hearing about his clean and sparkly upbringing, she could only imagine what he was thinking of her now that he'd seen Tulouse up close and personal. Thus far the visit home had been a complete waste of time thanks to a corrupt police force that had it in for her personally. And if that hadn't been bad enough, his consolation prize for all his trouble was a hard right hook by her felonious ex-husband. If he didn't blame her for this ordeal, it was only because he was a gentleman to the core.

Holding back a load of anger and frustration, she turned her face away and gazed out the side window, still not willing to accept his words of assurance. She wasn't sure if she should curse or cry, and just when a swell of tears readied to solve the debate, he gently took her hand in his and squeezed.

"Wade Griggs isn't your responsibility," he said, proving her assumption of him and driving a stake in her heart where her hopes and dreams should be.

Man, how she wished things were different. After spending this time with Rick then seeing Wade again, the truth became so obvious to her. All her life, she'd been looking for a hero, and as a young, stupid schoolgirl, she'd thought that hero was Wade. But he'd never held a candle to a man like Rick. Wade hadn't even earned the title. He'd just played football. And when times got tough, the true coward inside came out.

But here, holding the hand of a man who had every reason to be angry with her but offered comfort and support instead, she saw what a hero really was. And that realization scared the wits out of her.

He stopped at the corner and she turned and met his gaze, the loving look in his eyes putting all kinds of hazardous thoughts in her head. Stupid thoughts, like the two of them sharing a future, even though he'd made it clear that would never be the case. Maybe that was only a line he gave all the women he brought home. Maybe their time together had made him feel differently.

But in nearly five days, he hadn't uttered a retraction, and Jessie reminded herself she could be as ignorant as everyone else in this town.

All her life, her granna Hawley had instilled the belief that real heroes existed, that she would have seen it firsthand if her father hadn't died. Granna had worshipped the ground her son walked on and had promised Jessie that if she found herself a good, honorable man, she'd know how wonderful love and marriage and family really could be.

It was a nice fairy tale, one that got her through a turbulent childhood filled with disappointment. But by growing up, she'd gained more sensibility, she'd come to realize those ideals were nothing more than a lonely widow trying to keep the honor of her dead son alive.

Jessie was losing her heart to this tender, caring cop, thinking he might be that white knight she'd always dreamed of, and that meant it was time to put her head back on straight before she built up a big mound of heartache.

"No, Wade's not my responsibility," she finally agreed. "And I'd like to know for sure that he's not my husband, either."

He eyed her sympathetically. "Still no word from your lawyer?"

Turning her gaze back to the street, she worked to wall off the compassion in his eyes before she read too much into it. "No," she answered. "In fact, do me a favor and take a left at the next corner. His office is down the street. Maybe I need to show up in person."

Rick did as she asked, following her directions down a side street before pulling in front of the white-painted cinder block building that was the law office of Roger Blankenship. In the bright light of midday, she couldn't tell from the car if the office was open, but when she got out and read the sign on the door, she knew why her calls had gone unreturned.

His office was closed for the week. Family Vacation, the sign said in bright, shiny letters topped with a handmade smiley face. Which meant unless she found signed divorce papers at her parents' house, she wouldn't be able to clear this mess up until Monday.

She glanced at the car, noting that Rick was now talking on his cell phone, probably updating his partner on the big, fat dead end they'd run into. With nothing more for him here, he would probably go home now, maybe even get part of the drive out of the way today. If she were him, she'd be running from this place as fast as the speed limit would take her.

And she'd give anything to run away with him.

She started for the car, blazing heat bearing down on her and adding weight to her steps. Or was it the subject on her mind? She could go back with him to San Francisco and spend another night, maybe two in his bed. Maybe in that time she could start feeling him out, testing his resolve to stay a bachelor forever, maybe manage to change his mind.

And then every stern word of warning Georgia had ever uttered came back to her in full stereo sound. And Jessie couldn't deny her friend was right. It was true. Jessie did see the world through her grandmother's colored lenses. Her daydreams made her gullible, eternal hope made her vulnerable and attraction made her blind to lessons she should have learned by now.

And it removed all doubt that sometime before the day was out, she and Rick needed to go their separate ways.

Stepping to the car, she ducked into the passenger seat and closed the door just as Rick was shutting his phone off. He'd left the car and the air conditioner running, and she turned the vents toward her to chill off the heat. Reno had nothing on the hot August days of Texas, and she grabbed the neckline of her shirt and fanned away the sweat.

"My lawyer won't be back in his office until Monday," she said. "Right now, my last chance is that maybe the signed papers were sent to my parents' house. If not, I'll have to wait until he gets back to find out what happened to them."

Rick studied her for a moment before asking, "What if Wade's right? What if you're still married?"

It was the scenario she'd been trying to ignore all weekend, not willing to think until now that it could even be a possibility.

"I don't know," she replied. "Wade thinks that means half of everything I've got is his. He thinks that means I owe him fifty thousand dollars, but he's wrong there. Sure, Granna left me close to a hundred thousand when she died, but my mother guilted me out of half of that."

"You gave half to your parents?"

"I'm sure Granna turned in her grave over that, but yes. They were on the verge of losing their house. The restaurant Ray invested in was going belly-up and they were behind on the mortgage." She shrugged. "It's only money, but I did put the rest into my business and there's value in the co-op. I had to buy in, and there are people who would pay for my interest. The business has inventory. I rent, so he can't take my apartment." Just the thought of it all had her picking up her purse strap and fiddling with the beads. "I was strapped to the limit but on the verge of making it big before he showed up. If I have to start paying lawyers and selling off part of my business, I'll be back where I was a month ago, on the steps of IHOP asking for a job."

She leaned back in the seat and let the cool air brush over her neck. "It will be a setback, but I'll simply have to start over again. I built a successful business once, I can do it again."

"But in the meantime, you'll lose the momentum that magazine photo started."

"I probably already have. Saturday morning I was supposed to have been interviewing assistants. Requests were coming in for my bags and I've already lost a week of production time. I'm not going to kill myself working to make inventory if Wade's getting half the money I make. I won't do it, which means I'm not going back to San Francisco until I've straightened this mess out."

A flash of awareness registered in his eyes. It was the same one she'd had out on the sidewalk, that realization that the two of them were probably facing the end of this trip. She was already regretting it, but she couldn't tell by looking at Rick how he felt about it.

She forced herself to admit it didn't matter. Rick was a one-night stand that had turned into a five-day adventure, but it was nothing more than that. Besides, thinking about what she might be dealing with in the upcoming months was a sharp reminder that her life wasn't exactly at the best place for new a relationship.

She might be married. The thought made her shudder, but she had to accept it just as well. And if she was, she had a long, steep battle ahead of her that could cost her everything she had.

"This sucks," Rick blurted. And though Jessie couldn't deny that, she also wasn't going to strike up a pity party.

There was one thing she'd learned from her mother and Ray, and that was that life was full of second chances. Those two had lost and rebuilt so many times, it had kept Jessie's life in perpetual flux. But it also taught her that there was no such thing as giving up. When one door closes, you have to find a new one to open.

She forced a smile on her face, not willing to get sucked into the despair that tried to slink in from every angle. "It does suck, but I'll get past it. If I'm still married to Wade, it's my own damn fault for not following through like I should have. That's a lesson learned but not the end of the world." She pulled her seat belt over her shoulder and snapped it at her waist. "I'll just have to divorce him now, get out and start over again."

"You make it sound so easy."

She turned and saw a look in his eyes filled with more than sympathy for her situation, and Jessie remembered the wife he'd lost.

"It's not easy," she said, understanding tempering the tone of her voice. "But we don't have a choice, do we?"

They held each other's gaze for an extended beat, something passing between them that Jessie couldn't quite read. Or maybe it was all in her mind. When it came to Rick, she stood on shaken, unstable ground, hope trying desperately to take over and rule her heart. But she couldn't let it.

"What are your plans now that you've come all this way?" she asked, needing to push things forward.

He let out a long breath and stared at the phone in his hand. "Still nothing on the stolen car, but I did tell Kevin about Wade's claim to have been on a Greyhound. We're looking into that angle, checking all the routes that head into Banks. If he dumped the car for the bus, we might be able to find out what town it was left in."

The load she was carrying lightened. "So maybe driving all this way hadn't been for nothing?"

He quirked a brow. "I've solved cases on less. I never thought this trip was for nothing, even after meeting the honorable Chief Stott." Then another one of those looks crossed his face. "Besides, I had fun getting here."

The heat in his gaze flushed her cheeks. It came with

five days of memories flashing through her mind and prick- ling with sensation down to her toes. Her mouth curved and his lips twitched, both of them momentarily reliving every climax and intimate touch. It pumped a dose of anticipa- tion through her chest along with that pesky hope that kept rearing up and throwing thoughts in her head, like the idea he might suggest they keep seeing each other when they got back to San Francisco.

And then like that it was gone, his smoldering gaze iced over with the recollection of something that kept him from saying anything he might regret.

He blinked and cleared his throat, breaking the moment and releasing the tension between them. "I'm planning on heading back soon. What more do you need to do here?"

She sighed, then straightened in her seat. "I need to go to my parents' house. When I asked my mother about finding my divorce papers, she said we'd look when I got into town."

He pulled the car in gear and steered it out onto the street. "Then show me the way."

She brushed off the double meaning in that comment. Truth was, she'd give anything to show him the way. To help him get over his wife and learn to live again, to stop blaming himself for things he couldn't control, to hold on to that playful side she'd managed to reach in and yank out during their time on the road.

Jessie was the master at overcoming loss, and Rick was an easy case to take on. But the man wasn't asking, and her sensible side kept reminding her that people didn't accept help they didn't want, and that a one-sided love affair wasn't fun. So instead, she pasted a bright look on her face, shoved her feelings aside and led him to the place where they would say their final goodbyes.

16

RICK SPENT the ten-minute drive out to Jessie's parents' house embattled in a war between his gut and his brain. Hearing her say she planned to stay behind in Texas had hit him harder than that sucker punch from Wade, even though it shouldn't have. He'd known their trip together would end, that he and Jessie would ultimately go their separate ways and he'd return to his normal life. He just hadn't expected it would be today. He thought they'd have one or two more nights together. And he'd assumed that in that time he'd settle with the idea of them ending their affair. As if retracing the miles back home would somehow unravel the impression she'd made on him these last few days.

But Jessie had dropped the bomb on him, and while his brain kept insisting this was all for the better, his gut wouldn't shake the notion that after this trip, his life would never return to normal.

"It's this right turn up here," she said, pointing to a crossing where the road went from gravel to dirt. He made the turn, the noisy clattering of rocks kicking off his wheel wells giving way to a quiet roll of dust trailing behind them. In the distance he saw the white clapboard siding of a sprawling one-story ranch house, and a dusty gold Ford Taurus parked under the carport. As they approached, two old black

Labs came waddling out from behind an abandoned pickup truck, howling with the news that visitors had arrived.

"Dumb dogs," Jessie muttered under her breath, though her crooked smile said she was happy to see them.

A woman peered through creamy lace curtains at one of the windows. She had Jessie's face, but it was older and more tanned, framed in white-blond curls pinned up at the sides.

"Is that your mother?" Rick asked.

She nodded. "I'm glad she's home. She's usually out and about during the day and I don't have my key anymore."

Dry, yellowed lawn surrounded the house, accented by shade trees and a few sprawling bushes that didn't look to have been trimmed in decades.

"Park anywhere," she said, and after Rick pulled the car up behind the Taurus, she jumped out and called off the barking dogs. "Jake, Barney, get over here."

He stepped out of the car and found her scratching their ears while they nudged her chin with an affectionate welcome. One tried to pry his nose into her purse. "Sorry, no treats," she said, so they moved to Rick.

He raised his hands. "Sorry, nothing here."

The squeak of a screen door turned his attention to the carport where Jessie's mother stepped out, wiping her hands with a dish towel. She was short but trim, like Jessie, clad in a T-shirt, old faded jeans and purple cowboy boots that made him want to smile. Now he knew where Jessie got her fetish for color.

"It's about time you showed up," the woman said. "I heard you rolled into town over an hour ago."

He quirked a brow over the fact that news traveled so fast. Small towns like this were so foreign to him, he might as well be in India.

The two women hugged and shared greetings then Jessie turned to him. "Momma, this is Rick."

He held out a hand. "Pleasure to meet you, Mrs. Beane."

She looked him over good before accepting the handshake. "You can call me Marilyn," she said, her tone suggesting it was more an authorization than a welcome. He could see that lots of rumor, gossip and assumption was being calculated in those eyes right now, and what conclusions she came up with he could only guess. It didn't seem optimum, though, based on the guarded look in her eyes.

Releasing her hand from his grasp, she headed toward the house. "Y'all come in. I've made egg salad sandwiches."

Jessie gestured toward the house and they followed through the carport and into the kitchen, though he had to look hard to spot the appliances. The room had been decorated with floor-to-ceiling wallpaper printed in a glaringly bright garden motif. Flowery area rugs covered the linoleum in front of the sink and stove. Rows of fake carnations and ivy sat atop the white painted cabinets, which were adorned with porcelain knobs painted with pink tulips. And if that weren't enough, almost every spare wall held grapevine wreaths tied with bright country bows and more fake greens.

It looked like a flower shop exploded in the kitchen, and as he peered through the archway that led to the other rooms, he found more of the same.

"I've got Coke," Marilyn said from the open door of the refrigerator. "And there's beer for you."

"I don't drink," he replied. "A Coke is fine."

She looked back over her shoulder as if to be sure he wasn't joking, and when she saw he wasn't, shrugged and pulled out two colas.

He accepted the drink before taking a seat at the pine dinette table where she'd laid out a stack of white bread sandwiches, cut on the diagonal. Jessie put two halves on a paper plate and handed it to him before taking the seat across from him.

"Where's Ray?" she asked.

"Lubbock. Your cousin, Lorraine, has an office there selling insurance. I guess they're looking for more people and Ray's gone to check it out."

Jessie scoffed. "Ray's going to sell insurance?"

"Why not? If Lorraine can do it, Ray certainly can."

"I suppose."

As the two women caught up, Rick quietly sat and listened, eating sandwiches that ended up being unexpectedly delicious. He'd lived off restaurants for such a long time, he'd forgotten the simple pleasure of regular food.

"So I hear you're a detective," Marilyn said.

He nodded. "A homicide inspector, yes."

"You must be busy in a big city like San Francisco. I reckon you'll be needing to get back soon."

Jessie shot her mother an evil glare, but Rick wasn't offended by the question. Given what he'd seen of the town and the things Jessie had told him about her family, he hadn't planned on a warm, Texas welcome. In fact, the woman had been more polite than he'd expected.

"I'll be heading back today," he said, and already knowing the question in the woman's eyes, he added, "I'm just dropping Jessie off."

Marilyn brightened. She looked even more like her daughter when she smiled, and he found her age becoming. The years had drained away some of the baby fat that still adorned Jessie's face, raising those cheekbones and lengthening her chin, giving her a look he'd classify as more beautiful than cute. He wondered if that's what Jessie would look like in thirty years, and it stuck awkwardly in his gut when he reminded himself that he'd never know.

The woman pushed the plate of sandwiches toward him. "Have more. It's always nice to set out on a trip on a full stomach."

Jessie saw through the change in her mother's composure and from the look on her face, didn't like it one bit.

"I'll be going with him if those divorce papers are here," she said. "Did you have a chance to look for them?"

Marilyn patted her daughter's hand. "Now, Sugar, we don't need to air family business in front of strangers."

"Rick's not a stranger, Mom. He's a…" She paused, only for a moment, but it seemed like an eternity. What was he, exactly?

"He's a friend," she decided. "And he knows all about Wade and my divorce." She dropped her half-eaten sandwich on her plate. "I really need to find those divorce papers."

So casually, he almost missed it, Jessie's mother replied, "There aren't any papers, Sugar, and we can talk about this later."

His eyes darted to Jessie in time to see the blood drain from her face. "What are you talking about?"

"This isn't the time or place."

"It *is* the time and the place. What do you mean there's no divorce papers?"

Marilyn rose from the chair and took her plate to the trash. "You've lost your manners, Sugar. This isn't a subject to discuss in front of company."

"Rick's not company, Mom. He's driven me all the way to Texas. He's got as much right to hear about this as I do.

What's going on?" Then her voice rose with urgency. "Don't tell me Wade's right and we're still married."

The color was returning to Jessie's cheeks, but it wasn't a healthy glow. It was the flush of fury, and Rick grabbed a napkin and wiped his lips. "I can leave you two alone."

Jessie held up a hand. "No, you don't." Then she turned to her mother. "Tell me Wade and I are divorced."

All sound and movement stopped. It was as if the life had suddenly been sucked from the room.

Marilyn eyed him reluctantly, then Jessie, before leaning against the counter and letting out a huff. "Three days after Deloris died, Roger called and said Wade had a change of heart. He didn't want the divorce and wasn't going to sign."

Jessie flew from her seat, the chair screeching across the linoleum as she rose to her feet. *"Why didn't you tell me?"*

"Now, Sugar, there was too much going on. You were beside yourself over your granna's death and everything you went through after Wade got arrested. It wasn't the time to make decisions about anything."

"So you just decided to keep this to yourself? For a *year?*"

"I'm sorry, Sugar, but I have to agree with Wade. You both needed some time to think things over." She shook a scolding finger at her daughter. "Marriage isn't something you just toss aside, you know. You two had been through a lot. You weren't thinking clearly."

Jessie looked as if she was about to burst into tears, and Rick wouldn't blame her if she did. "Mother! Wade was thinking clear as day! If he didn't sign those papers it was only because he'd found out about the inheritance."

"No one had read the will by then."

"But he wasn't an idiot. Everyone knew I was Granna's

only heir." Jessie lowered back to her seat and put her head in her hands. "I can't believe you did this. I can't believe in this last year, you didn't tell me. *How could you?*"

"You know I was against this divorce from the start."

"It wasn't your decision."

The sound of despair in Jessie's voice tore a hole in Rick's heart. Every part of him wanted to step over and wrap her in his arms, but he knew that would be the worst move he could make.

"This isn't the time or place, Sugar Beane," Marilyn said, her voice taking on an edge that let Rick know he needed to leave the two women alone.

Grabbing his Coke, he rose from the table. "I've got some calls to make. I'll be outside."

The gesture garnered no apparent appreciation from Jessie's mother, who no doubt wished he'd get in his car and drive away for good. But he wasn't going to leave Jessie like this.

Placing a hand on her shoulder, he lightly squeezed.

She didn't raise her face from her hands and he had to tear himself from the room, wishing like hell he could pick her up and bring her with him. The sentiment shook him, and for the first time since they'd left San Francisco, he realized he needed to take a hard look at his feelings for her.

Stepping outside, he saw a large upturned bucket under a tree and walked over to take a seat. The air was thick with heat and dust, but in the shade he found relief. It didn't take the dogs long to come to his side, and he looked into their eyes, wishing those sober gazes could tell him what to do in this situation. There was no mistaking the emotion in his chest. It had been percolating since he first saw her at Scotty's Friday night, and it now had come to a full boil.

He was falling in love with Jessica Beane.

Or should he say Mrs. Wade Griggs?

He looked over at the house where he knew her mother was trying to convince her to come home and put her marriage back together. Not that he believed she would. Jessie was too smart to be conned and too strong to be a pushover.

But was she strong enough to add the love of a man like him to her long list of problems?

He wanted like anything to walk into that house and carry her away, but he knew reality never played out as easily as his dreams. What would life really be like once they got back to San Francisco, back to his job and the tragedies he dealt with every day? How would he feel once he returned to all the things that reminded him of the wife he'd lost?

This trip had made it easy to set reality aside, but how could he guarantee smooth sailing and loving bliss once they returned to the real world?

He couldn't. In fact, he couldn't guarantee that life with him would be much of an improvement over the one she was trying to leave behind. Of course, Rick was no felon, and he'd never lay a hand on her, but that didn't make him a saint. He still had a mountain of emotional garbage to sift through, and the woman in that house had had enough garbage thrown at her for one lifetime. She didn't need more.

Despair clogged his throat and he tried to clear it by giving the dog a friendly scratch. "You're what she needs, buddy boy. Unconditional love and friendship without all the baggage." The dog scooted closer and licked his chin, and just as the other began to whimper for attention, he heard the slam of the screen door.

He rose to his feet as Jessie came storming toward him, her face red with anger and her eyes glassy with emotion.

And when she moved within reach, he pulled her into an embrace, burying her face in his chest and holding her close to his heart.

"I'm sorry," he said, bending to kiss the soft curls on the top of her head. He sucked in a breath, wanting to soak in that sweet scent of berries and sunshine until it swept through his lungs and mingled with his blood. He could have stayed like this forever. Though his heart was heavy with the knowledge that this would be the last time he'd have his arms around her, but she pulled away and wiped her thumbs over her eyes.

"How could I be so stupid?"

"Don't go there."

"I can't not. What kind of idiot doesn't follow through to make sure her divorce is final?"

"You had a lot going on."

She laughed bitterly. "And that should have been on top of my priority list." Placing her hands on her hips, she turned and took in the view of the grassland surrounding the house. "Momma swears against it, but I can't shake the feeling that she led me to believe it was handled. I could have sworn I'd asked if those papers had been sent to their house. She said she wouldn't lie, but I know my mother. She has ways of dodging the truth and making insinuations." She shook her head. "I should have known better."

He shoved his hands in his pockets. "Trust me, because I've got a lot of experience at this. Don't waste your time second-guessing what you should have done."

She studied him knowingly. They'd only talked briefly about Natalie's death, but he could see by her expression she understood.

"I won't," she said, the anger and frustration in her voice

beginning to temper. "Lord knows, it's not the first stupid move I need to get past. This marriage was one I thought I'd taken care of, though."

"You'll take care of it now."

She nodded, and when they both knew there wasn't much else to say, the smile slid from her lips. She held her gaze on his for two, three beats, her eyes expressing thoughts and sentiments he couldn't read. He wanted desperately to ask what was going on in her mind, but he was too afraid to, knowing that with the slightest suggestion, all his resolve to end this relationship would be out the door.

But he had to stick to his plan. Jessie deserved better than he could give. So instead, they just stood and stared, until finally she broke the silence.

"I need to stay in Tulouse and look after this."

A vise gripped around his throat. "And I need to go."

The words broke the lock between them, and she dipped her eyes to the dirt. "I'm sorry for all this. I wish we'd found your car. Those poor parents—"

He pulled his hands from his pockets, stepped close and gently cupped her face, drawing her gaze back to his. "Don't take that on, either. That wasn't your fault."

She swallowed hard and touched her hand to his. "You're one of the good ones, Sheriff."

"Maybe sometimes," he said, holding her face in his hands and wishing like hell he could kiss her. But he knew if he did, he wouldn't stop, and certainly wouldn't let go.

Even hot and dusty she was the picture of a fresh spring day, those strawberry curls hanging like spun ribbon around her cheeks, those ripe, red lips plump and glossy and those big brown eyes perpetually bright and brimming with fire. He wanted to bend down and taste her one last time, and absorb everything that was true and good about her until it all rubbed off on him.

If he only knew for sure that his gloom wouldn't rub off on her instead.

She gently patted his hand at her cheek then pulled from his grasp. "I should grab my clothes from your trunk. I'm sure you're anxious to get out of this town now that your business is done."

He cleared his throat and yanked the keys from his pocket. "Yeah, sure." And with tension mounting between them by the second, he helped her gather her things then awkwardly stood beside his car.

He wasn't sure what to say or do. These nights together seemed to warrant something, but with the only words coming from his heart off-limits, there wasn't much left. What he really needed to do was go back home and make a solid effort at working through his problems. If he'd learned anything from the sexy cowgirl in front of him, it was that life was meant for living, and he knew now that he'd been dead for too long.

Though he didn't know how, he needed to start the process of healing, and for that, he wished he could thank her. But the words simply wouldn't form.

So he stood there, waiting like a dope until she stuck up her chin and smiled. "On your way back through Reno, you should pick up that Road Runner."

A little of the tension eased and he laughed, having forgotten all about the car. "They've probably sold it by now."

She shrugged. "You never know. Sometimes things are meant to be."

Before he could search her eyes for meaning behind the comment, she stepped up and kissed him lightly on the cheek. "Thanks for the ride, Sheriff. You have a safe trip home." Then she backed away toward the house.

Just like Jessie. Always making everything easy for him. Even an uncomfortable goodbye hanging in the hot air between them, loud and messy from all the words they weren't speaking, had been cleaned up by Jessie, leaving a nice, shiny path for him to make his escape.

And like the coward he was, he took it.

"Thank your mother for me, will you?" he asked.

Based on the way she huffed he knew it was going to be a while before she said anything to her mother, much less thank-you. And it was a quick reminder that he was doing the right thing by leaving. His presence would only exacerbate an already bad situation, and he wanted to help, not hurt her more.

So as he said one last goodbye, slipped behind the wheel of his car and started the long drive back home, he repeated to himself that leaving was the right thing to do.

If only it didn't feel so wrong.

FOR A LONG TIME Jessie stood on the driveway, watching the road as Rick disappeared out of sight and the remnant dust cloud settled over the fields. She'd thought parting ways with him now would have spared her the pain of getting attached later. But it had already come too late. Somewhere during the last five days, she'd gotten herself hung up on the sexy cop. And once again she'd managed to throw her heart out where it didn't belong.

She blamed her granna's ideals and her own relentless optimism. It was that joining of forces that had her believing crooks were good guys and that good guys could somehow fall in love with her during one quick road trip.

Dumb, boneheaded, fairy-tale thinking, dreamed up by a little girl who desperately wanted her father back and the grandmother who assured she'd find a new man she could count on someday.

"Sorry, Granna," she mumbled. "That doesn't seem to be working out for me."

Maybe someday it would, but right now, standing on a dry, dusty field in west Texas, Jessie was totally and completely alone.

The depth of it weighed on her shoulders and hung heavy in her chest. Stepping over to the bucket where she'd found Rick sitting under the shade, she sat down and wondered if she truly had the strength to see herself through this latest disaster.

Despair gripped her. Less than a week ago she was on top of the world, living in a bustling cosmopolitan city, her fashion business on the verge of taking her to all kinds of exotic places. She'd had steamy, red-blooded sex with a hot, handsome cop and was prepared to walk away with plenty of chips on the table and her heart intact.

And now, only days later, she was back in Tulouse, still married to a criminal who had the power to destroy her dreams, surrounded by a town that blamed her for their troubles and a family that had their own ideas about what kind of woman she should be.

And with her granna gone and her one friend back in California, she didn't have a solitary soul on her side.

A cold nose nudged her arm and she looked down to see Barney, those black eyes telling her he was here for her. At least until Ray got home and put out his dinner.

She accepted the gesture anyway, thanking the companionship with a friendly scratch behind the ears while her eyes swept back to the road ahead. The silly, hopeful side of her kept thinking that silver sedan might come rolling back like the shiny white knight of her dreams. But Rick was in the next county by now, on his way back to deal with troubles of his own. And the longer Jess stared at the empty, quiet road, the more she came to terms with the fact that there would be no shining saviors this time around. This time, without Georgia or Granna or Darlene or Rick, she would truly have to pull herself up, dust herself off and find her own way to achieve her dreams.

And with the overwhelming burden holding a tight grip on her fears, she stood and began the slow process of setting it aside. She hadn't room to waste energy feeling sorry for herself or pining over what might have been. This time around, she'd need all the energy she could get if she wanted to keep hold of the life she'd started.

She just hoped that would be enough.

17

"I CAN'T BELIEVE you did this." David Marshall stood in his driveway, scratching the gray hair on his head while his blue eyes teetered between shock and delight.

"I figured Mom got that Avalon she'd been wanting for years, you deserved a toy of your own," asserted Rick. He opened the driver's-side door to the lime-green Road Runner and held out a hand. "Check it out. It's exactly like the one you had when I was a kid."

From behind Rick heard his mother's gasp. "It's the Green Monster! Where did you find it?" She stepped hurriedly to the car to get a closer look.

Rick watched as his mother, dressed in her typical pale chinos, white polo shirt and tan driving mocs, circled the car, her wide mouth agape.

"I was in Reno this weekend and a couple there was displaying it for sale."

His dad rounded the car and eyed him disbelievingly. "So you bought it?"

Rick had to admit, this type of impromptu purchase had never been in his nature before, but seeing the delighted looks on their faces, he was glad he did it. He hadn't been the only one devastated by Natalie's death, and it was time the family shared some joy for a change.

"It hadn't exactly been my idea. I was there with a friend," he explained. "And when I told her the story about us owning one and why you sold it, she suggested I buy it." He shrugged. "I couldn't find a reason not to."

His mother raised a hopeful smile. "She?"

For over a year now, Rick's mom had been less than subtle about her desire for him to start dating again, and it didn't surprise him that she hadn't missed the remark.

"Just a friend, Mom."

The twinge in his gut had him changing the subject. "It's got the 440+6, Dad, almost four hundred horse. It'll do 120 like nothing."

That veered his mother's attention back where he wanted it. "Don't tell me you drove it that fast!"

He shrugged and eyed his father knowingly. "Nevada's got some long, deserted straightaways."

"Which means it could have been weeks before they found your body."

"Oh, Paula, you worry too much," his father chimed in.

"And I'm not an inexperienced teenager anymore," Rick added. "Which means Dad should have his old muscle car back."

His father looked up at him. "You seriously bought this car for me?"

"What am I going to do with it in the city? Besides, I can always come take it for a drive when I want to. That's one of the conditions. I get to drive this one." Then he shoved his hands in his pockets and smiled. "Consider it an early birthday present."

A swarm of touching emotion came over his father's face. Rick had never really done anything like this for the old man before. It felt good to spread some happiness, to offer his father a gesture of love and give the two of them something that would bring them together again. For a number of reasons they'd gradually distanced over time, and this car held the promise to change that trend.

And this was all Jessie's idea.

He quickly dismissed the thought, not caring to ruin what was the first good feeling in his heart since he drove out of Tulouse four days ago.

If there'd ever been an event to match the heartbreak of losing his wife, leaving Jessie behind in Texas had come in second. The drive home had been restless and wrought with uncertainty and debate. He wanted desperately to believe he'd done the right thing for both of them by leaving when he did, but all the logic and reasoning in the world wasn't crushing the idea that they needed each other.

For sure he needed her. She'd been the only woman since Nat who'd instinctively known every right move to make at exactly the right time. She hadn't put up with his moods, hadn't allowed him to slink into his familiar grumbling gloom. And in the middle of it all, Jessie had opened his eyes to the living, breathing world around him, reminding him that he was still a part of it no matter how badly he wished he weren't.

And above all that, she'd never tried to compete with his dead wife, or set out to try to fix him.

Jessie was just Jessie, her hands full enough with her own disappointing past, she wasn't about to carry his, too.

And damn if that wasn't exactly what he needed.

But what can you give back to her?

That was the question that paralyzed him, the one that kept him fearing that he was being selfish with her heart. Watching his parents together in their near little house, enjoying their life of retirement with the two children they'd raised, he wondered if he could share this with Jessie. Since his wife died, he'd never been able to shake the feeling that this was *Nat's* family, the place where *she* was supposed to be, the grandparents of *her* children and not anyone else's. This had been their life, and bringing someone else into it would feel like second best.

And Jessie deserved better than second best. She deserved to be the entire sum of someone's heart, living in a space created just for her.

So as badly as he wanted to sweep her off her feet and bring her home to him, he couldn't stop the nagging impression that he would be getting more than he could give.

His father slapped his back, and the melancholy instantly disappeared. "Let's see what this puppy can do," he said.

Rick nodded and held out the keys. "I buy, you fly."

THE TWO MEN were on Interstate 280 and halfway to Mountain View before Rick's father shot him a sideways glance. "So tell me more about this friend you went to Reno with."

Rick sighed. "Can I utter the word 'she' without you and Mom running me to the altar?"

"I'm only wondering what kind of woman could talk you into buying your dad a muscle car."

"She didn't talk me into it. She suggested it. I thought about it for a few days and decided it wasn't a bad idea."

"Well, I'm glad you did." The man smiled. "I don't know why I hadn't thought about doing something like this before. I guess we just get wrapped up in our day-to-day lives and forget about the things we used to enjoy."

Then he flicked his brows at Rick before shifting down and adding, "And I used to enjoy my power cars."

A space had cleared to their right and his father stepped on the gas to pass a BMW that had already been doing eighty in the fast lane, and when they flew by, the Beemer's driver tapped his horn in friendly admiration.

The honks and grins and thumbs-up from other drivers had always been one of the fun parts of owning a classic car, and with plenty of open road ahead of them, his dad laid into it, the rush of speed putting smiles on their faces and laughs in their chests. Rick couldn't remember when he and his father had been out on the road for a drive like this. He would have been sixteen or seventeen, he guessed. Too long a time to pass for two men who had always been close.

Both being cops for the San Francisco PD, Rick and his father shared a bond that spread over several facets of their lives, a bond that had worn down with the tragedy of losing Nat. But it felt stronger than ever right now as they sped down the highway.

It felt like freedom, and happiness and old times with the first friend Rick had ever come to love. And when he considered that this was all thanks to Jessie, something broke inside him and he found himself spilling all the details of his week to his dad.

Rick told his father about finding Jessie in the bar, about his stolen car, the Anna Mendoza case and his suspicions about Creed Thornton. He confessed to losing the evidence, and driving all the way to Texas in the hope of getting it back. But mostly, he talked about Jessie, about the way she made him smile, the way she'd reacted when he'd told her about Nat, and the way his heart turned in his chest every time he was around her. He explained her problems with Wade, told him about the run-in with the local police and the business she was on the verge of losing.

And then, with his chest heavy and his voice rough with emotion, he confessed to his father that he'd fallen in love with her.

Without uttering a reply, the man turned off at Crystal Springs, driving along the waterfront to Highway 92 toward the coast at Half Moon Bay. He brought the car down to the speed of traffic as they trolled along the two-lane highway through the marshy grasslands and wooded hills, and once they'd settled in to the flow behind a blue Dodge Caravan, he finally said, "I didn't think I'd ever hear you say those words again."

His voice was tinged with something that sounded like hope. "I'd sure like to meet this woman. She sounds pretty special."

Rick shook his head. "I'm a mess, Dad. And she's got a mountain of problems of her own to sift through. I keep feeling like I'd just be adding one more problem to the mix."

His father sat silent for a moment, the only sound between them the rumble of the muffler and the low hum of the engine. Then he said, "She sounds like a sharp woman, based on the way you describe her. She'd have to have a good head on her shoulders to start up a business and make it successful."

"That she is."

"She also sounds like she's got a solid backbone, standing up to the locals to do what she felt was right."

It was one of the things Rick was most proud of. Jessica Beane had more strength and guts than some of the toughest people he knew, and working the SFPD, he knew quite a few.

"Then why are you treating her like she's too dumb to decide if she wants to be with you?" his father asked.

The question caught Rick off guard. He'd just been interrogated by his retired cop father.

His dad shrugged, the exact way he would have back on the force, dressed in a suit, holding a cup of coffee and coming in for the kill with a guilty suspect on the verge of confessing. "Didn't you say the first night you'd met her you told her what she was in for, then left the decision to her?"

"Yeah, but I'd only been protecting my conscience."

"Now you're protecting her," his dad said, nodding as though it was the biggest line of BS he'd ever heard.

And maybe it was. Maybe Rick was being a coward, afraid to commit to the task of getting over his dead wife and making a new life for himself. Maybe inviting Jessie into his life meant he'd finally have to pull the trigger on his past with no option of going back. And maybe the reality of that scared him speechless.

"Just something to think about," his father offered.

He circled back up the highway, the conversation moving to sports and small talk as they enjoyed the return drive to San Mateo. It was early evening by the time they pulled into the driveway, and his mother insisted he stay for dinner, bringing her baked beef Stroganoff out of the oven to seal the deal.

Their one-story traditional was very similar to the house he and Nat had been looking to buy before she was killed, and that was one of the main reasons he didn't come here as often as he should.

It hurt too much.

Watching his father and mother work together in the kitchen, setting out the plates and gathering drinks from the fridge—it had been too painful a reminder of the life he was supposed to be living with his wife right now. But after spending the afternoon with his father, talking, confessing, laughing and enjoying the day, Rick realized he was tired of living in pain. He'd been wallowing in self-pity for so long, it had become second nature, and only since Jessie did he really feel the calm that came with letting the past go and accepting those things he couldn't control.

It was frightening, but also exhilarating, and it was a feeling he didn't want to lose.

Why not let her decide?

His father's words had kept ringing in his head as Rick tried to find an answer. But there was none. His dad was right. Jess was a grown woman with a sharp mind and loads of resilience. Instead of treating her like a child, he should do what he did that first night they met—lay it on the line and let her decide if she wanted to take a chance.

But would she?

Truth was he didn't even know what kind of dreams Jessie had when it came to love and romance. They'd only talked about her career, one she was on the verge of losing as quickly and painfully as he'd lost his wife. He had no idea what she'd do once she divorced Wade, but if she were willing, maybe the two of them could build new dreams together. Not replacement dreams—fake replicas of the lives they'd lost— but new ones, made special for the two of them here and now.

He didn't know if she'd want it, but did he have the guts to at least try?

As he sat down to share a meal with his parents, he resolved to give it thought once he was at home. For now, he was going to appreciate time with the people he hadn't seen enough of over these last couple of years.

But as he took the first delicious bite, his cell phone rang. Looking down, he moved to pull it from his pocket.

"Now, no phones at the table," his mother scolded. "It's a family rule."

He eyed the number, saw it was Kevin and rose from the table. "I'm sorry, I need to take this."

Stepping through the dining room, he flipped open his phone when he reached the front living area. "Yeah," he said.

"The tip about the Greyhound panned out," Kevin said, his voice high and quick with excitement. "We found the car."

A surge of adrenaline sped through his veins. "Where?"

"Flagstaff, Arizona. It's in an impound lot, towed for being abandoned under an overpass. And you'll never guess what the local PD found in the trunk."

Rick brushed a hand through his hair and checked his watch. "How fast do you think I can get there?"

"By morning for sure. You might be able to find a red-eye out of SFO."

"I wonder how early the impound lot opens."

He could hear Kevin's smile in his voice. "Doesn't matter. I explained the situation and the Flagstaff PD has offered any assistance you need. They'll open the lot whenever you get there, and they're holding the laptop in evidence for you."

Rick's heart hammered in his chest. It had been a good day that was only getting better, and it was about time.

"Kevin Fong," he said, so thrilled he wanted to jump and high-five the sky. "I think our luck is finally changing."

18

"HOW ARE THINGS at the shop?" Jessie paced her parents' family room as she and Georgia caught up on what had been happening during her week in Texas.

"Your inventory's almost sold out, Jess. I've put the last of your supply on the shelves. There's only five or six purses left and a couple of belts and when those are gone you won't have anything. Oh, and there's a stack of phone messages. I've called most of them back and told them you had a family emergency and are out of town, but that will only hold them off for a while. When will you be home?"

Jessie ran her fingers through her hair and sat down in the sofa chair as her stepbrother Trip barreled in. He plopped on the couch and grabbed the remote to the television. He was wearing the same baggy jeans and John Deere T-shirt he had on the day before, and based on the smell, she guessed he hadn't washed them in between.

Of her two stepbrothers, she'd always found Trip the most revolting.

"In a day or two," she replied. "I've got a meeting with Roger tomorrow. He'd needed some time to pull my file and go over the original divorce settlement. I think once I meet with him, the rest can be handled from San Francisco."

At least, that's what she hoped. She'd been in Tulouse

only a short while and was already climbing the walls. She'd forgotten how small this house could be with her two brothers still living at home, even though both were pushing thirty.

Trip flipped on the TV and popped the cap on a can of Old Milwaukee. Foam bursted over his rough, callused fingers and threatened to spill on her mother's hunter-green carpet. Quickly he raised the can to his mouth and sucked off the liquid while upping the volume on MTV.

"What's that noise?" Georgia asked.

"Trip just came home."

"Tell him I said hi."

Jessie referred to her brother. "Georgia says hi."

He responded with a long, rumbling belch.

"Nice," she muttered, rising from the chair in search of a quieter place to hold a conversation. When she'd reached her old bedroom, now converted to a sewing room, she shut the door and sat down on the wrought-iron daybed.

"This place is driving me crazy. Ray's talking about renting an apartment in Dallas while he goes through some insurance training school. They've already spent the money I gave them. Mom's going to have to go back to her job at Reeds to afford a house and an apartment, which isn't sitting well with her. Meanwhile, the boys are eating them both out of house and home."

"Sound like nothing's changed, then."

"Only that R.J. has a job now, but if he's giving anyone money, Mom's not seeing it. At least it gets him out of the house during the day."

Jessie looked out the window and spotted the dogs asleep under a tree, their fat bodies spread out like two globs of black tar in the grass. "It's *so* time for me to leave."

"When do you see Roger?"

"Tomorrow, and unless he's got a really solid reason for me to stick around, I'll be taking the next bus out of here right after."

"That's good. We need you here. I didn't tell any of the partners what's going on. You know how they are. Swan would start a panic if she thought you couldn't come up with rent. She'd get the four of them on a tangent. They were fine with my excuses a few days ago, but now that your stock is almost gone, they're getting antsy."

Jessie smiled that there was one person she had still looking out for her. "I appreciate you holding down the fort. I promise to call you the minute I get out of Roger's office tomorrow. I'm already looking into bus schedules and might even splurge on a flight if Roger gives me good news." She lay back on the bed and tucked a pillow behind her head. "I should be back tomorrow night or Thursday at the latest."

"Looking forward to it, hon. You call and let me know."

"Will do."

She snapped her phone shut and stared up at the popcorn ceiling, still not believing she'd ended up in her old room after everything that had happened. When she'd left she hadn't expected to ever come back for anything other than a holiday or a family event. And even then she'd sworn she would have gotten a room at the Lamplighter before spending another night in this house.

Amazing, what a difference a day can make.

Tossing the phone on the bed beside her she studied the rough texture of the ceiling, looking for shapes or faces like she used to do. She had to admit that of the places they'd lived, this house had been her favorite, and she was pleased to see her parents hadn't lost it. Yet. In high school, she used to lay here and daydream, and over the last few days, she'd done the same, trying hard not to let those thoughts wander to Rick. Though against her will, they always did.

She wondered what he was doing. Had he met with that poor couple, or was he holding off, still hoping to find something they could use to put their daughter's killer in jail? Had he gone back to Scotty's, had he bought a new car yet and was life for him going back to the usual grind?

And, most of all, was he ever thinking of her?

If she closed her eyes and concentrated, she could almost feel him. What she'd give to run her fingers over that sinewy chest one more time. To taste the salty essence of his skin, breathe in that musky scent and feel those strong arms wrapped around her. She'd loved the weight of him on top of her, and the way he gasped and shuddered when he fell apart inside her. His hot breath against her neck had warmed her and those lips had made her burn. And despite all the sex they'd had over their five nights together, she'd felt as though it was barely enough.

It was amazing how a man could leave a woman sated and hungry all in one shot, but that was the way she felt with Rick. And now that their affair was over, she wondered if she'd ever find a man who would match what she'd had with him.

The ring of her phone pulled her from her thoughts, and she reached over and checked the number.

It was her lawyer.

Anxiously she flipped open the phone, hoping this un-expected call meant he had good news.

"Hello?"

"Sugar, it's Roger. I've got some papers for you to sign and wondered if you had a minute to drop by."

Confusion pursed her brow. "Papers to sign? What papers? I thought we would talk things over in our meeting tomorrow."

There was a long, strange pause before he said, "I figured you wanted to get back to California sooner than later. I've got the time if you do."

This didn't make sense, but she wasn't going to argue. Spending the afternoon divorcing her husband was a way better option than lying in her old bedroom staring at cobwebs and pining over a man she'd never see again.

"I'll be there in ten," she said, then flipped off the phone.

Her mother had gone out, but in the kitchen, she found the keys to Trip's truck and took off without asking to borrow it. He would have objected and she didn't want to hear it. Besides, she was too distracted by this turn of events. The situation made only stranger when she pulled in front of the white brick building and saw a county sheriff's cruiser parked in front.

Grabbing her purse, she jumped down from the truck, stepped through the glass doors and into the reception area.

"Hey, Sugar, long time no see," said Pearl, Roger's assistant. Pearl had always been kind to Jessie, and she smiled to see that situation hadn't changed.

"You, too. Nice to see a friendly face."

Pearl's smile held plenty of understanding. She motioned for Jessie to follow her to the conference room, and when she opened the door, the sight left Jessie shocked and confused.

Sitting around the large table was Roger, Sheriff Chaney, the man who had been in charge of the criminal investigation against Wade, a third man she didn't recognize, and...*Rick.*

The minute she spotted him, her heart leaped quickly, his crooked grin creasing that sharp jaw and those deep blue eyes filled with charm. And with the wind sucked from her lungs, she could only stand there and stare, her mouth bobbing while she took in the people and wondered what was going on.

Roger waived a hand. "Sugar, come in. You're just in time. Have a seat."

On shaky legs, she moved to the nearest chair, set her purse on the table and looked at the men who were seemingly pleased to see her.

She took in Sheriff Chaney, an older man with dark, bushy eyebrows and a perpetual day-old beard. Once he'd determined Jessie hadn't been involved in Wade's affairs, he'd been the one man in law enforcement to stand steadfastly beside her, ordering everyone in the sheriff's department to treat her like the victim she was.

Jessie had grown to like and respect the sheriff, and when he smiled and nodded, "Nice to see you again, Sugar," she replied with a warm grin.

Roger introduced the man she didn't recognize as Mr. Ortega, Wade's parole officer with the county.

"Ms. Beane," he said in greeting, and Jessie instantly liked him for not referring to her as Mrs. Griggs.

Then she eyed Rick, his open expression filling her with wonder and anticipation. Eventually she was able to ask, "What's going on?"

Roger gestured toward Rick. "Inspector Marshall called me about your divorce yesterday. Apparently there's been a turn in events with regard to Wade's parole." Then gesturing toward Sheriff Chaney and Mr. Ortega, he added,

"He's been working with Colbrook County regarding some charges Wade's facing in San Francisco, and—"

He was cut off when the conference room door opened and Wade was escorted in by Pearl. "Here you are, Mr. Griggs," she said, then turned to Roger. "Can I get you refreshments?"

Roger shook his head. "No, thank you, Pearl."

And when she closed the door, Wade stood at the end of the table. "What the hell is this?" Glancing at his parole officer, he asked, "Why did you send a cruiser to pick me up? I haven't done anything. And what are we doing here? This is Sugar's lawyer, not mine."

"Have a seat, Mr. Griggs," Roger invited.

"I'll stand," he said defiantly.

A second county patrolman stepped in and stood next to Wade, and Jessie noticed he was casually holding a pair of handcuffs.

"Mr. Griggs," Mr. Ortega began. "Inspector Marshall is here from the San Francisco Police Department."

"We've met," Wade spat.

"Then you know he's been trying to trace a stolen vehicle."

"Look, I don't know what this guy told you, but—"

"The vehicle was recovered," Rick cut in. "And it's got your fingerprints all over it."

Jessie squeaked, not able to stop the thrill from slipping from her lips, though the all-business look in Rick's eyes never wavered.

"This is a setup—" Wade started, but neither Sheriff Chaney, Rick nor Mr. Ortega had any interest in hearing his defense.

"Obviously, you've violated your parole," Mr. Ortega stated, motioning to the patrolman who slipped a handcuff on one of Wade's wrists before he could attempt to back away. "You're being extradited to San Francisco to face charges of grand theft auto, not to mention the problems you'll be facing here in Colbrook County."

"He's got nothing," Wade attempted.

"We've got the evidence we need to prove you stole the car. We've got a pawnbroker in Reno who will testify to giving you payment for goods stolen from Ms. Beane's San Francisco apartment. And since you transported stolen goods across state lines, we'll be calling the FBI about possible federal charges."

Wade looked around the room with panic in his eyes. There was no one here to defend him. Captain Stott certainly couldn't protect him now, and this time there were no locals here to rally around him and cry foul.

Wade was totally screwed.

Though Jessie knew she should be the better person, she couldn't help feeling elated at seeing Wade's chest pump with distress. Terror was slowly setting in as he realized he was going back to jail.

"However, as the primary in this case, I'm willing to drop the charges if you're interested in cutting a deal," Rick offered.

That got Wade's attention.

"What deal?"

Rick turned his attention to Roger, who answered for him. "I've drawn up papers that will sever the marriage between you and Sugar, here. If you're willing to sign them, Inspector Marshall will drop all charges with regard to the stolen vehicle and the theft that took place back in San Francisco."

Jessie's jaw dropped.

"I divorce the bitch and I go free?" Wade asked.

Sheriff Chaney rose from his seat, his jaw clenched and his gaze threatening. "Watch your language, Mr. Griggs."

"What's the catch?"

"No catch," Roger said. "You sign away your rights to anything Sugar acquired after your separation eighteen months ago, and same goes for her. She's not entitled to anything you might have acquired since then."

Wade shot out a scoff. "All I acquired was prison time."

"Justifiably," Jessie mumbled.

"This is blackmail," Wade shouted. "There's a law against—"

Rick stood. "Go ahead and book him. We're wasting our time." Then he pulled his phone out of his pants pocket. "I'll see how quickly we can get the FBI out here, or I can handle that after he's been extradited to San Fran—"

"No, wait!" Wade ground his teeth and curled his lip at both Rick and Jessie. He knew he had no way out.

Roger pushed the papers and a pen toward Wade, and after surveying everyone there and coming to terms with the idea that he hadn't any choice, he muttered an obscenity, grabbed the pen and signed.

Pearl came in shortly after to notarize both their signatures, and with the matter settled, Roger held out a hand to Jessie. "Congratulations. You're officially divorced." They shook hands. "I'll have these couriered over and filed with the county right away."

"Actually I'd like to ride along and see that happen in person," Jessie said, having her fill of trusting others when it came to her divorce. Though it felt as though the weight of an eighteen-wheeler had been taken off her shoulders, she wasn't leaving this town or this state until she had the papers in her hand. Not to mention a second set in a safe-deposit box, and confirmation from every legal professional she could find that she was truly, unequivocally divorced.

Everyone rose except Mr. Ortega, who told Wade they still had business to discuss, and leaving the two of them behind, Jessie said her thanks and goodbyes and stepped out into the August heat, soaking it in like a warm, friendly bath.

Rick stepped out beside her, and even though their affair was supposed to be over, she let out a squeal, jumped into his arms and planted that sexy mouth with a long, sloppy kiss.

He slipped his arms around her and held her tight. With a deep kiss on her mouth, he locked their hearts and bodies together.

"Mmm," she moaned, not wanting the moment to end. The tingling sensation of his touch prickled across her skin. She hadn't believed she'd be in his arms again, and even for just this moment, she settled to take what she could get for as long as she could have it.

She brushed her waist against his, the hardness behind his fly getting her more hot and bothered under the baking Texas sun. As his strong hand caressed the base of her spine, she feared any more of this and she'd combust right there on the sidewalk.

He broke the kiss. "I missed you."

The unexpected sentiment filled her heart. "How can I ever thank you? Do you know what you did for me there?"

The loving affection in his gaze poured through her. "Well, if I'm going to have a shot at a future with you, I need you divorced."

She blinked. "A what?"

Taking her hand, he led her a few paces from the door and into the shade of a large ash. "I know what I said the night we met, but I'd like to take it back."

"Take it back?"

He nodded. "I'd like more than a couple of nights with you." He shifted and took both hands in his, lifting her fingers to his lips and pressing them with a warm kiss. Then his eyes went somber.

"Look, Jessie, I need to be honest with you, like we've been from the start." He swallowed hard and went on. "I've got a lot of pain in my past I need to get over. I'm not the easiest guy to be around. I can be a grump and the job makes me moody sometimes."

She nodded as he spoke, not as much in agreement, but in answer to what she hoped he was about to ask.

"I can't promise you bliss any more than I can wish my hurt away. But I can say this for sure." He kissed her fingers again. "I want to come back to the living. I want to start thinking about a future. I want to put my past in the past and start looking ahead. And I want all that with you."

Something like hope or happiness exploded inside her. "Yes," she said, but her throat was so tight with emotion, only her lips mouthed the word.

"I'm ready for it now," he said. "It's time for me to move on."

"Yes," she said again, but this time it only came out as a hoarse whisper, too faint for his ears.

"And whatever it is you're looking for in a career, in a family, in your life, it's all open for discussion. I just want a—"

"Yes!" she finally blurted, the word coming out louder than she expected after trying so hard to break her vocal chords free.

"Yes?"

"Ye—"

And right then, she heard the squeak of the door and those damnable boots again. "Oh, look at this," she heard Wade say from over her shoulder. "My slut wife in the arms of—"

But Wade didn't finish the sentence. Before Jessie could blink, Rick had nudged her aside, reared back and shot his fist square into Wade's jaw, sending him flat on his back faceup on the sidewalk.

"That's *ex*-wife, you jackass!"

Rick stood over him, shaking out his hand and breathing hard, only partially holding back a smile as his eyes beamed with long overdue satisfaction.

Sheriff Chaney stepped out after him, and Wade held his chin and cried, "That son of a bitch just hit me!"

"Actually, I think Wade tripped on the sidewalk," Jessie said, pointing to a spot where the ash tree had uprooted the pavement.

Chaney looked down and scratched his head. "Oh, yeah. I could see where that might be very dangerous."

Wade pulled himself up to his feet, touching his hand to his cheek. "He hit me. Knocked me to the ground. I'm pressing—"

"Wade Griggs," the sheriff said, "I think you've found yourself in enough trouble today. It's time to leave these poor people alone."

And with Wade's protests fading off behind them, Rick led Jessie toward the quiet of a shaded spot around the corner.

"That felt good," he said.

She laughed. "It felt good to watch."

When they'd strolled far enough down the block, he reached into his pocket, pulled out something shiny and stopped. "I think this is yours," he said, placing her father's stolen medal in her hand.

Tears welled in her eyes and she touched her fingers to her lips and gasped. "You found it."

"Under the seat with a couple of other things."

She swallowed. "And the laptop?"

He nodded. "It was all there."

And as she looked down at the gold emblem in her hand, the green and white striped ribbon still attached, she sobbed for her granna, who'd known the truth all along.

You were right, Granna.

Heroes really *did* exist, good guys did win and Jessie had found herself one that she intended to keep forever.

"We didn't get to finish what we were talking about back there," he said. She looked up into those sizzling blue eyes that always made her insides do a fast somersault.

"About you being a grump and hard to live with?"

He chuckled and nodded. "That, too."

She laced her arm in his and started walking again. Clutching her father's medal tightly in her hand, she felt the freedom of all her troubles behind her and a future filled with love.

"You'll be a piece of cake, Sheriff."

Epilogue

One year later

RICK STOOD on the steps of San Francisco's Hall of Justice, holding court behind Captain Jameson. Kevin, Rick's partner, stood alongside. Nearby were Paolo and Lucy Mendoza. They were answering questions from a press anxious to hear their reaction to the guilty verdict that had just been handed down to Creed Thornton in the murder of Anna Mendoza.

"Clearly we are pleased," the captain said. "And we are all thankful Mr. and Mrs. Mendoza have finally found justice for their daughter's murder."

"Captain Jameson," one reporter called out, holding a microphone high in the air. "How did your unit make the connection between Creed Thornton and Arthur Begley, the man he hired to stage Anna's suicide?"

Rick tightened his jaw, knowing the captain wouldn't tell them his hacker friend in the Haight had managed to unlock a series of e-mails between Creed and his old college roommate, who had already been listed as a suspect in an unrelated crime. None of the evidence on the laptop had been mentioned in the files, and as far as anyone knew, it had never been recovered from Rick's stolen car.

But it had caused Rick and his partner to go back through Creed's past, making a list of all the people he'd been associated with over the last decade. And when Arthur Begley popped up as a suspect in abetting battery, they had the excuse they needed to legitimately make the connection between the two men.

"Thorough police work," the captain said, "and a little luck."

A round of laughter added to the celebration, and when the interview was done, Rick ducked away from the crowd to where his future bride was waiting for him, having just arrived from a business trip to Paris.

Her bright smile was like the cherry topping on an already wonderful day, and he scooped her into his arms and pressed her lips with a welcome-home kiss.

"Congratulations," she sang, all dressed up in a crisp white tank top and bright orange denim pants, one of her Beane Belts slung low on her waist, surrounding her in a sparkling kaleidoscope of beaded color.

"Couldn't wait for you to get home." He kissed her again.

"Paris was dull without you, but I'm glad I got back in time to hear the verdict." She looked over her shoulder at the Mendozas who were sharing their reaction with the press. "They look happy."

Rick nodded. "As happy as they can be."

He didn't have to say more, knowing Jessie already understood that this day could only give them so much. It was one of the things he loved most about her.

His loss of Natalie still hurt. It was something that would never go away. But thanks to Jessie and the new life they were putting together, the pain was fading and he was learning to live in the second chapter of his life.

It was a good one, filled with new hopes and dreams with a woman who loved him, and a woman he loved back with all his heart. Thanks to Jessie, he'd learned there was room for more than one love, and he intended to share that love with her for the rest of his life.

"So did you scope out a honeymoon in Paris?"

She shook her head. "I'm thinking wedding and honeymoon in Reno. We'll take the Green Monster. We can get married by Elvis. I'll buy a shirt that says 'Trophy Wife' and we'll show off the car during Hot August Nights."

He laughed, wondering what his mother would think of that, then realizing his mother was thrilled just to see him happy again. His mother and Jessie had hit it off easily. Jessie was finally getting that caring family she'd always dreamed of, and Paula Marshall was finally getting her son back.

"Plus," she said, "it would be a shorter drive for Ray and Momma."

He looked down into her sweet honey eyes. "You think they'll come?"

"Of course, they'll come. It's a wedding, after all."

He slipped his hand into hers and walked her toward his car. "Then Reno it is, if you're really serious."

She laughed and shrugged. "I don't know. We'll see." Then she looked up at him, a calm ease settling over her smile and those eyes filled with pride. "I am happy to be yours," she said.

"The luck is all mine, babe," he said, kissing her lips. "It's all mine."

* * * * *

Here is a sneak preview of
A STONE CREEK CHRISTMAS,
the latest in Linda Lael Miller's acclaimed
McKETTRICK *series.*

A lonely horse brought vet Olivia O'Ballivan to
Tanner Quinn's farm, but it's the rancher's love that
might cause her to stay.

A STONE CREEK CHRISTMAS
Available December 2008
from Silhouette Special Edition

Tanner heard the rig roll in around sunset. Smiling, he wandered to the window. Watched as Olivia O'Ballivan climbed out of her Suburban, flung one defiant glance toward the house and started for the barn, the golden retriever trotting along behind her.

Taking his coat and hat down from the peg next to the back door, he put them on and went outside. He was used to being alone, even liked it, but keeping company with Doc O'Ballivan, bristly though she sometimes was, would provide a welcome diversion.

He gave her time to reach the horse Butterpie's stall, then walked into the barn.

The golden retriever came to greet him, all wagging tail and melting brown eyes, and he bent to stroke her soft, sturdy back. "Hey, there, dog," he said.

Sure enough, Olivia was in the stall, brushing Butterpie down and talking to her in a soft, soothing voice that touched something private inside Tanner and made him want to turn on one heel and beat it back to the house.

He'd be damned if he'd do it, though.

This was *his* ranch, *his* barn. Well-intentioned as she was, *Olivia* was the trespasser here, not him.

"She's still very upset," Olivia told him, without turning to look at him or slowing down with the brush.

Shiloh, always an easy horse to get along with, stood contentedly in his own stall, munching away on the feed Tanner had given him earlier. Butterpie, he noted, hadn't touched her supper as far as he could tell.

"Do you know anything at all about horses, Mr. Quinn?" Olivia asked.

He leaned against the stall door, the way he had the day before, and grinned. He'd practically been raised on horse-back; he and Tessa had grown up on their grandmother's farm in the Texas hill country, after their folks divorced and went their separate ways, both of them too busy to bother with a couple of kids. "A few things," he said. "And I mean to call you Olivia, so you might as well return the favor and address me by my first name."

He watched as she took that in, dealt with it, decided on an approach. He'd have to wait and see what that turned out to be, but he didn't mind. It was a pleasure just watching Olivia O'Ballivan grooming a horse.

"All right, *Tanner*," she said. "This barn is a disgrace. When are you going to have the roof fixed? If it snows again, the hay will get wet and probably mold…"

He chuckled, shifted a little. He'd have a crew out there the following Monday morning to replace the roof and shore up the walls—he'd made the arrangements over a week before—but he felt no particular compunc-tion to explain that. He was enjoying her ire too much; it made her color rise and her hair fly when she turned her head, and the faster breathing made her perfect breasts go up and down in an enticing rhythm. "What makes you so sure I'm a greenhorn?" he asked mildly, still leaning on the gate.

At last she looked straight at him, but she didn't move

from Butterpie's side. "Your hat, your boots—that fancy red truck you drive. I'll bet it's customized."

Tanner grinned. Adjusted his hat. "Are you telling me real cowboys don't drive red trucks?"

"There are lots of trucks around here," she said. "Some of them are red, and some of them are new. And *all* of them are splattered with mud or manure or both."

"Maybe I ought to put in a car wash, then," he teased. "Sounds like there's a market for one. Might be a good investment."

She softened, though not significantly, and spared him a cautious half smile, full of questions she probably wouldn't ask. "There's a good car wash in Indian Rock," she informed him. "People go there. It's only forty miles."

"Oh," he said with just a hint of mockery. "*Only* forty miles. Well, then. Guess I'd better dirty up my truck if I want to be taken seriously in these here parts. Scuff up my boots a bit, too, and maybe stomp on my hat a couple of times."

Her cheeks went a fetching shade of pink. "You are twisting what I said," she told him, brushing Butterpie again, her touch gentle but sure. "I meant…"

Tanner envied that little horse. Wished he had a furry hide, so he'd need brushing, too.

"You *meant* that I'm not a real cowboy," he said. "And you could be right. I've spent a lot of time on construction sites over the last few years, or in meetings where a hat and boots wouldn't be appropriate. Instead of digging out my old gear, once I decided to take this job, I just bought new."

"I bet you don't even *have* any old gear," she challenged, but she was smiling, albeit cautiously, as though she might withdraw into a disapproving frown at any second.

He took off his hat, extended it to her. "Here," he teased. "Rub that around in the muck until it suits you."

She laughed, and the sound—well, it caused a powerful and wholly unexpected shift inside him. Scared the hell out of him and, paradoxically, made him yearn to hear it again.

* * * * *

Discover how this rugged rancher's wanderlust is tamed
in time for a merry Christmas, in
A STONE CREEK CHRISTMAS.
In stores December 2008.

THE MISTLETOE WAGER

Christine Merrill

Harry Pennyngton, Earl of Anneslea,
is surprised when his estranged wife,
Helena, arrives home for Christmas.
Especially when she's intent on
divorce! A festive house party
is in full swing when the guests
are snowed in, and Harry and
Helena find they are together
under the mistletoe....

*Available December 2008
wherever books are sold.*

REQUEST YOUR FREE BOOKS!

2 FREE NOVELS PLUS 2 FREE GIFTS!

HARLEQUIN®

Blaze™

Red-hot reads!

COMING NEXT MONTH

#435 HEATING UP THE HOLIDAYS
Jill Shalvis, Jacquie D'Alessandro, Jamie Sobrato
A Hunky Holiday Collection
Santa's finally figured out what women want—hot guys! And these three lucky ladies unwrap three of the hottest men around. Don't miss this Christmas anthology, guaranteed to live up to its title!

#436 YULE BE MINE **Jennifer LaBrecque**
Forbidden Fantasies
Journalist Giselle Randolph is looking forward to her upcoming assignment in Sedona…until she learns that her photographer is Sam McKendrick—the man she's lusted after for most of her life, the man she used to call her brother….

#437 COME TOY WITH ME **Cara Summers**
Navy captain Dino Angelis might share a bit of his family's "sight," but even he never dreamed he'd be spending the holidays playing protector to sexy toy-store owner Cat McGuire. Or that he'd be fighting his desire to play with her himself…

#438 WHO NEEDS MISTLETOE? **Kate Hoffmann**
24 Hours: Lost, Bk. 1
Sophie Madigan hadn't intended to spend Christmas Eve flying rich boy Trey Shelton III around the South Pacific…or to make a crash landing. Still, now that she's got seriously sexy Trey all to herself for twenty-four hours, why not make it a Christmas to remember?

#439 RESTLESS **Tori Carrington**
Indecent Proposals, Bk. 2
Lawyer Lizzie Gilbred has always been a little too proper…until she meets hot guitarist Patrick Gauge. But even mind-blowing sex may not be enough for Lizzie to permanently let down her guard—or for Gauge to stick around….

#440 NO PEEKING… **Stephanie Bond**
Sex for Beginners, Bk. 3
An old letter reminds Violet Summerlin that she'd dreamed about sex that was exciting, all-consuming, *dangerous!* And dreams were all they were…until her letter finds its way to sexy Dominick Burns…

www.eHarlequin.com

HBCNM1108